PENGUIN

MURDER

F. X. Woolf is the pseudonym of a well-known crime novelist.

Murder
IN SPACE

Adapted by F. X. Woolf
from a screenplay by Wesley Ferguson

Penguin Books

Penguin Books Ltd, Harmondsworth, Middlesex, England
Viking Penguin Inc., 40 West 23rd Street, New York, New York 10010, U.S.A.
Penguin Books Australia Ltd, Ringwood, Victoria, Australia
Penguin Books Canada Ltd, 2801 John Street, Markham, Ontario, Canada L3R 1B4
Penguin Books (N.Z.) Ltd, 182–190 Wairau Road, Auckland 10, New Zealand

First published by Penguin Books Canada Ltd, 1985

Printed and bound in Great Britain by
Cox & Wyman Ltd, Reading

Canadian Cataloguing in Publication Data

Woolf, F.X.
 Murder in space

ISBN 0-14-008370-7

I. Ferguson, Wesley. Murder in space. II. Title.

PS8595.054M87   1985   C813'.54   C85-098641-9
PR9199.3.W66M87   1985

Murder

IN SPACE

CHAPTER ONE

"Conestoga, this is Mission Control. Do you read us? . . . Conestoga, this is Mission Control. If you read us, please respond on Laser Transmission System, frequency Niner-Six-Niner-Five . . ."

The man in the striped pajamas looked at the monitor with a newly opened eye. If looks could kill. If machines could die. But that was exactly what McCallister was waiting for: had the machinery up there died and with it its human cargo? Bare feet on the floor found battered slippers, and the middle-aged man got off the bed and reached for his robe. In its bright colours, he looked younger again, but as he moved in and out of the long shadows, his age seemed to change like the readings on a VU meter.

"Conestoga, this is Mission Control. Do you read us? . . . Conestoga, this is Mission Control. If you read us, please respond on Laser Transmission System, frequency Niner-Six-Niner-Five . . ."

McCallister looked at the familiar face with its walrus moustache, and the red marks made by his glasses on each side of his undistinguished nose. Was he losing more of his remaining hair, he wondered. He tightened a cheek muscle and let it pass.

He tried not to look at the lines of care and worry on his face as he shaved, but they were there: purplish stains under his eyes, new lines that hadn't been there the last time he'd looked. Nine weeks? Can nine weeks do that to a healthy man?

From the window he could see the sun just starting to rise over the eastern horizon. In the distance, shadows stretched long fingers to the reddish-gold mountains. It had been snowing again. It was 6:09 a.m.

As he tightened the laces of his Adidas, feeling the lift that always gave him, he heard the monitor again begin its mournful call into the void. He looked at the clock radio by his side of the empty bed. He hadn't listened to his usual morning programs for nine years, even though the calendar testified that it was only nine weeks since McCallister had had this extra dollup of stress added to his normally heavy-pressure routine.

"Conestoga, this is Mission Control. Do you read us?" McCallister shut off the monitor as he left the bedroom. He would be out of touch for half an hour. "Thank God for small mercies," he muttered and he walked past the refrigerator and the coffeemaker on his way to the back door.

The station wagon wound its way through the familiar streets of the university campus. The snow was melting and running off into the gutters. McCallister thought the wagon could probably find its way by itself after so many years. He took a final puff on his cigarette and ground it out in the overflowing ashtray in the dashboard. Now only the radio and the remaining smoke in the car kept him company as the fraternity houses and the new chemistry building sailed by. McCallister had taken his first degree in chemistry, and for an instant, he remembered the smell of the labs and the echo of the lecture hall in that far-away eastern campus. Jeffrey Kilbride, the network's indefatigable news hawk was on the radio with the overnight news. McCallister pictured Kilbride as he adjusted the tuning.

"Good morning. This is Jeffrey Kilbride with the news. First, a Conestoga update. It is now the beginning of the ninth week since the space mission under the command of Captain Neal Braddock lifted off the surface of Mars to begin the journey back to Earth . . ."

"Shit, as if I need him to remind me," Mc-

Callister said aloud through the windshield. Kilbride continued:

". . . Nine long weeks in which, inexplicably, there has been no contact with Mission Control from the nine international scientists and astronauts who undertook this unprecedented and dangerous journey a scant five months ago."

Kilbride was right. The time had gone quickly until the line went dead up there. Since that date there'd been nothing. Kilbride's broadcast this morning contained nothing new, just the round number: nine. Nine weeks without a word. No wonder it was difficult for the Civilian Director of the Conestoga Space Mission to look his colleagues in the eye. He took a pack of cigarettes from the dashboard and lit a fresh one. The news report continued.

". . . Following lift-off from the Red Planet, Mission Control picked up intermittent low-level electronic signals, indicating that the Space Laboratory is indeed headed for home — but the lack of communication from those aboard remains a mystery."

The station wagon rounded the curve by the Olympic stadium, behind the athletics building, and came to a stop. McCallister, looking like an out-of-condition walrus in his shapeless blue jogging suit, kept his hand on the keys waiting for Kilbride to finish before turning off the ignition. ". . . As of last night, observers at Palomar have isolated a moving object which may or may not be the Space Lab. If it is, then Conestoga would only be three days away from Earth and possible re-entry *if* — and these are big ifs — the object is indeed the Conestoga, *if* the craft has not been disabled in some way — and *if* their three-week encampment on Martian soil has not led to some physical or mental debility that would preclude the space travellers' safe return to Earth. This is Jeff —" McCallister snapped the radio off. If a flick of a wrist could make an editorial judgment, McCallister's just wiped Kilbride off the face of the earth. But he had to admit, grudgingly, as he shifted his weight out of the car, Kilbride had got the essentials right. And, until the moment they made contact with the errant Space Lab, there was not much even the director of the mission could do, except worry and wait.

McCallister took his first turn at a fast walk around the track with his cigarette still clenched in his teeth. He had gone to the track initially to get his wife and his doctor off his back. If his arteries benefited at all, that was a bonus. As he began the second lap, he adjusted the headphones over his ears more carefully. Life is a series of fine adjustments, he had discovered, and now the Mozart was flooding into his inner ears in perfect stereo.

Before the first movement was developing the second theme, a car, a black unmarked car, pulled to a stop beside McCallister's wagon and killed its lights. As the driver spotted the jogging figure, the lights were turned on again to the bright position, and the car mounted the curb and roared towards the moving figure on the track, far from the stadium. The car sped down on McCallister, who was still listening to the music and his own pounding heart. The car changed its angle to catch McCallister. The horn honked steadily as the car came to a stop ahead of the runner, skidding in the cinders of the track.

McCallister, deaf to anything but the music, stopped suddenly, as a man jumped out of the car and rushed up to him excitedly.

"What the —?"

"Dr McCallister! We've got 'em! We've got 'em!" McCallister quizzically pulled one of the earphones away from his ear. "We've got 'em, Doctor! We've made contact!"

CHAPTER TWO

The International Space Exploration Administration, the ISEA, was an impressive cluster of modern steel and glass buildings, featuring prominent slabs of curved white concrete. The complex covered more than two snow-laden acres, and in the crisp early morning sun, it glistened like an ice palace.

At the heart of the ISEA was the Mission Control Complex, and its Civilian Director, Dr Andrew McCallister, was already moving quickly down its long corridors — towards the heart's heart, the main Communications Center. No longer in his track blues with the word *Colorado* across the chest, McCallister had changed into his perennials: the unpressed sports jacket, open-collared light shirt, and nondescript trousers. McCallister was his tailor's worst advertisement. He hated neckties and formality but kept both at hand in case they were needed.

The tall, pinch-shouldered, dark-haired man at his side was filling him in. "We picked 'em up around 6:20. The audio's okay, the picture's crap but they think they can fix it."

McCallister grunted, moving his face so the Einstein-like moustache shifted expressively. "Who's been advised?"

"The President, the Secretary." Mitch Carlino spoke matter-of-factly; he was nominally ISEA's Director of Security and looked strictly Harvard Business School in his three-piece suits, but, as McCallister knew, was in reality a CIA agent. "And Rostov, of course," Carlino added with a small sigh.

"Which means the world'll know by breakfast," growled McCallister, as he calculated the tactical cost. "Before we've had a chance to debrief."

Carlino tried to speak lightly. "Can't be helped," he shrugged as McCallister swore.

"Hell with it. At least they're still alive."

The two men passed through a doorway and into the Communications Center. "We have a discrepancy in your TJ thrust. I have us at seven-four-three-six negative." The voice came from the direction of a huge TV screen that dominated one wall of the room. The speaker, Captain Neal Braddock, was a flickering, now faint, now distorted, image on the screen. He was reporting to one of the dozens of technicians sitting at the room's central computer console.

"I cannot confirm that, Conestoga," said the ground technician slowly, as if speaking to his aged, slightly deaf mother. And even more slowly, "We will recalculate."

McCallister glanced round the room. The Communications Center was arranged in a horseshoe of computer terminals and display units, each station occupied by a variety of young experts, to whom the flashing lights and buttons meant the difference between order and chaos in a technologically based world where there were no ambiguities.

With Carlino following, the Director walked to the centre console. The technician slid over, making room. McCallister, Carlino thought, could feel like an avalanche moving your way in slow motion.

McCallister leaned into the microphone. "Neal," he said, as if he'd have to hear the answer himself before believing it.

"Hey, Andy." The face on the TV screen flickered a slight smile. "You're up early." Braddock sat, almost lounged, in his chair, the top of his blue tunic open revealing a red shirt beneath. He looked like the captain of a successful football team of a decade past. He had fair hair, receding slightly, and a strong, mobile face.

"What the hell happened?"

Braddock's answer had the kind of steely

casualness that means to say 'I'm in control.' "We got swamped by a meteor shower two days after Mars lift-off," he said. "Wiped out communications and we're off trajectory." In case his audience didn't get the point, he added quickly: "Nothing we can't fix."

"What about your standby equipment?" McCallister asked.

"Same problem," said Braddock. "Too much interference."

McCallister's growl seemed to wait a minute before finding words. "You're pretty goddamn casual about it."

"You know me, Andy. Grace under pressure." That flickering smile came over the screen again.

"Everyone okay?" McCallister asked.

"Fine. Major Steiner and Pam Cooper are on EVA trying to goose up our reception."

"What about fuel? You have a major course adjustment coming up in twenty minutes."

"Ask our navigator."

A wavy-haired, good-looking young man replaced Braddock on the screen. David Tremayne was smiling.

"Morning, Doctor. It *is* morning down there, isn't it?"

"Sure is," said McCallister, smiling back in spite of himself. "Good to see you. Our computers say your fuel situation could be better."

Tremayne winked. "Tell your computers we're okay."

"They'll be glad to hear it."

McCallister suddenly felt a nudge, and turned to find Carlino at his side.

"Rostov," Carlino whispered, then blew a silent whistle.

"Tell me something I don't know," said McCallister, just as the stocky Russian liaison officer reached him. Rostov's ever-present smile was not meant to be friendly; it was meant to express its own falseness. The Russian was attached to the space project because he was deputy administrator in the Soviet space program — and because he was a KGB officer.

"This is wonderful news, Doctor," Rostov said to McCallister, taking in the rest of the room, touching McCallister lightly on his upper arm as McCallister put David on hold. "Communication at last." He sort of sung the words. "You are to be congratulated."

McCallister had stepped back, as if stung. "Afraid I have nothing to do with it."

Still smiling, Rostov moved quickly to the point, "Has there been any damage to the ship?"

"We're running tests now. Apparently not."

"They are well?"

"Yes," McCallister spoke as if to end the matter. He well knew the endless number of ways Rostov could find to ask the same question.

"My government will be very happy, particularly our Commissar Denerenko, who has been understandably worried about the safety of his wife. I would like to speak with Colonel Kalsinov."

It was Carlino who answered: "In time."

"Oh, come, come," said Rostov. "For nine weeks my people have been worried about their countrymen. Surely I can be spared a few moments."

McCallister, turning to the screen, made quite sure that Rostov felt the meaning of his heavy sigh. He spoke into the mike, to David: "Captain Braddock —"

"I'll get him, sir," young Tremayne answered, moving off the screen as Braddock reappeared.

It was Rostov now leaning into the microphone. "Good to see you, Captain. I am relieved to know you are all safe and well."

"Thanks." Braddock spoke guardedly.

"Neal," McCallister now stepped in, "if you haven't already been briefed, several weeks ago Russian Premier Savarnych was deposed and his successor named Olga's husband to serve on the Politburo."

"I know. Mitch Carlino filled me in and Olga has been notified."

The screen was suddenly crowded, David Tremayne returning with a third man whom Rostov immediately greeted, but in Russian.

"In English," Carlino spoke coolly to Rostov. "You know the rules."

"Ah," said Rostov, practically bending at the knee, "forgive me."

The third man was Colonel Andrei Kalsinov, famed cosmonaut, hero to his people.

"Colonel Rostov," he said, "it's good to hear your voice."

"I trust you are well," said Rostov.

"Yes, I am fine, as is Olga Denerenko. She is delighted by the news of her husband's appointment," he said, speaking guardedly.

"And the mission," Rostov asked. "Has it been satisfactory?"

Kalsinov spoke deliberately. "What I have to say should wait until my return to Earth. At that time I will provide you with a detailed report on our activities."

There was a pointed silence, then Rostov shattered it. "Yes, I see. I look forward to it with great interest."

Carlino looked at McCallister. McCallister was looking at Rostov, then back to Carlino. None of them looked happy.

CHAPTER THREE

The inside of the ISEA Mission Control Complex was a series of galleries and walkways overlooking the central communications room. McCallister's own office looked down on this area of concentrated work with its horseshoe of computer terminal stations through windows which managed to muffle the sounds of activity in the room below. Footsteps echoed down one of these walkways, as McCallister, straining to keep up with Carlino, headed in the direction of his office.

"Cryptic exchange," Carlino was saying. "Our friendly KGB bastard is playing his usual games."

McCallister grinned wryly, "Unlike our CIA bastard." Carlino's face reddened.

"What are you trying to do, blow my cover?" Before he got a chance to reply candidly about the political games being played between periods of the scientific games, McCallister stopped dead in his tracks.

"Oh, Christ!"

Carlino failed to discover the source of his boss's annoyance. "What is it?"

McCallister nodded his head in the direction of the anteroom of his office, where a well-groomed, polished, familiar face was waiting. "Kilbride." Carlino rolled his eyes towards the ceiling-hung blower unit, and smiled. "Look, Mitch," McCallister continued, "I don't want this place overrun by the press, not until I get a complete report from Braddock." Carlino nodded, and wore his serious expression. "Tighten security. Nobody gets access unless they've been cleared through you." Carlino added another nod to the set and moved off, as McCallister continued towards his office.

Jeffrey Kilbride moved quickly as he saw McCallister come into the anteroom. He was in his mid-thirties and smiled with the assurance of a man who knows he stands among the top three in the network ratings. He was the quintessential anchorman, McCallister thought, half matinée idol, half department store floorwalker.

"Great news about Conestoga, Andy. What was the problem?" Kilbride found that standing in McCallister's path was dangerous work. The Director swept past him, muttering, "Technical. You'll be filled in." When he reached the desk of his secretary, Dinah Greenberg, he leaned across the desk.

"Dinah, put me through to the President."

"Yes, sir."

Dinah began to place the call, but not without first checking to see whether her boss required further assistance with Kilbride. In the ten years she'd spent as McCallister's girl Friday, she'd grown fiercely loyal to the Director, and had gone through her thirties running interference for him with pillars of the media like Jeffrey Kilbride. McCallister made a move towards his office door. Kilbride played his best card: a friendly arm across McCallister's shoulder, and added to that the tone of one who is used to sharing the secrets of state, accustomed to confidences at the highest level.

"Look, Andy," he began, "I hear the video transmission's uneven but we've got to get some coverage out to the country." He flashed his familiar "state of the union" look at McCallister who had seen it too often to be undermined by it. "How about setting up an interview right away with a feed to the networks?"

"The networks. Plural. Nice touch," thought McCallister, but he said, "Can't do it. Maybe tomorrow . . ." Kilbride's face reddened.

"Tomorrow? Christ . . ." The anchorman realized that he was running out of control. He caught his breath, grinned and tried again. "Andy, if we wait, people will start asking questions."

McCallister stared at him. "Only if you put the thought in their heads." Then he lowered his tone and bent in the direction of confidentiality. "Look, Kilbride, I've got scientists up there and right now it's all I can do to just keep this mission together. Tomorrow," McCallister said through firm lips that told it the way it was. "Maybe." He punctuated his last word with a direct look into the reporter's eyes that told him that "Maybe" was as good as he was going to get.

McCallister broke off the conversation at that point and entered his office, closing the door firmly behind him. Kilbride hesitated, weighing his desire to know more, to get at the secret that in a few moments the Director would be discussing with the President, against the knowledge that McCallister had beat him down again. Dinah could see his anger simmering as he stood there, rooted to the spot where McCallister had left him. Without a word, he turned and left the anteroom. Dinah watched him go as the light on her direct line lit up her board.

"This is Mission Control. Dr Andrew McCallister calling the President," she said.

McCallister's office was a combination of things. If it weren't for the view through tall inside windows down to the floor of the Communications Center, it could have been the sanctum sanctorum of a Midwest college president. A large table lamp on his desk helped to take the impersonal sting off the large room, joining the carefully selected chairs and couches in making the Director's office into a living space if not quite a livingroom. McCallister's family looked out at him from a silver frame on his desk. Curtains and broadloom completed the effect. At his desk McCallister was going over some letters. He looked at them, but without really seeing them. There was only one thing on his mind this morning: the nine scientists up there. Matters of invitations to embassy receptions and the renewal of requests from publishers were abstractions he was unable to deal with today. The buzzer of the intercom sounded. Glad of the chance to return from contemplation to action, the Director leaned across his desk and flipped the switch. "Yes, Dinah?"

"Sir, I have the *Vice*-President coming on line one." For a moment McCallister hesitated. He hadn't anticipated talking to the Veep.

"Right," he said at length, and lifted the receiver. "Good morning, Mr Vice-President."

"Hell, yes, it's good. Wonderful news, Andy. We're told everyone's just fine."

"Yes, sir." The Veep had that special political magic about him, a way of talking to millions and making each of that vast audience think it was a personal conversation. McCallister had watched, admired, and yes, envied the Veep this gift. It worked even across the miles between them.

"I know how hard you worked putting this mission together, Andy," he said. "The Chief and I are both delighted the crisis is over."

"I appreciate that, sir, but we may still have a problem." McCallister heard the intake of breath over the line as the Veep reacted. McCallister continued. "Something's going on up there. Maybe I'm reading between the lines — and maybe I'm paranoid — but the Russians might be planning to throw us a curve or two."

"Specifics?" This was the other side of the Veep. He knew when to smile for the cameras and when to cut the crap. McCallister could picture the Vice-President listening intently at his end of the line and making notes.

"There are no specifics. Nothing yet. Maybe just some negative propaganda. We'll have to deal with it when it happens." McCallister wished he had something more solid for Washington, but he had said his piece, or most of it. "Oh — and my other problem is the media. They want access to the Space Lab — some kind of network coverage."

"Indulge them, Andy," the Veep chuckled over the phone, every inch the political animal who had clawed his way out of big-city ward politics. "Let them have their broadcast. Meanwhile, I'm flying up this afternoon. It's an election year and the Chief wants us to hog a little of your glory. You understand?"

"Hog all you like. You're entitled." The receiver quivered in McCallister's hand as the robust laugh of the Vice-President crossed the continent.

"Talk to you when I get in," the Veep said.

"And as for the Russians — screw 'em." There was a pause while the politician reflected on this off-the-cuff remark. "Did I say that?" he said, sounding like a schoolboy caught out in a fib. "Bye, Andy." McCallister heard the click as the line went dead, and grinned to himself as he lowered the receiver.

CHAPTER FOUR

"Control, I read you at Vector Niner-Niner-Six-Four-Two. Do you copy?" The voice, with its clipped English syllables, belonged to Pamela Cooper, missions computer systems expert. David Tremayne stood by her side, and Braddock paced the command deck, as all three waited for confirmation from Mission Control. Now was the moment for making the final adjustment in their trajectory.

The grey form of the Conestoga moved through space with solidity and the appearance of sureness. It appeared to be almost a minor object of the solar system going about its diurnal business according to some law of nature rather than the plans of a group of earthbound politicians and scientists.

At last: "We copy, Conestoga. Prepare to fire Forward Stabilizer Rockets Seven and Eight. Counting down: ten — nine — eight —"

Tremayne was flipping switches on the mini-computer. Repeating: "Seven, armed. Eight, armed."

"Fuel level, six-four-three," Pamela intoned; then, "Set ignition."

Tremayne reached to the switch at the top, right-hand side of the panel. "Ignition set."

"Simultaneous fire . . ." Pamela pushed one, two buttons, "*now*." And as the craft lurched, leaving Braddock balancing on one foot for an instant, Pamela moved quickly to activate the system — one, two, six buttons pushed — and Tremayne raced to another computer, throwing on a second string of switches.

"Control, we have fired," Pamela said calmly. "Repeat, we have fired."

"We copy," came back from Mission Conrol.

Like the other eight astronauts, Pamela Cooper wore the same blue uniform, with national flashes on the right shoulder. Hers were British. Her blonde hair was tied in a neat chignon, her complexion and fine features spoke of England's heralded green and pleasant land.

Pamela got up and moved to a computer read-out screen at one end of the Command Deck. She pressed a button and watched, as a red line appeared on the screen, crossing the grid design in a parabolic arc. A second line, in green, flashed below the red line. Its path was similar, yes; but not identical. Braddock had moved to Pamela's side, and both watched the screen intently.

It was like the final minutes in a chess match.

"Control." Tremayne was making contact again. "I have computer confirmation on lateral attitude — Alpha George five-five-one-one."

And as the radio voice came through, "Confirming five-five-one-one," Pamela and Braddock watched the green line move to the red one. Closer, closer. Until it stopped.

"We've got it, sir!" Pamela had broken into a delighted grin, and Braddock squeezed her shoulder. He spoke softly, smiled slowly: "Helps to be lucky, doesn't it?"

The youngish man with a dark moustache was peering into a microscope. He grunted with a kind of contempt for what he saw.

"You've found something," said the woman at his side.

"Take a look." Guy Sterling, the Canadian civilian in charge of the ship's science lab, moved out of the way for his assistant. Even as she peered into the microscope eyepieces and frowned, it would be clear to anyone that Dominica Mastrelli was a beautiful young woman. Dark hair, white skin, broad and flat cheekbones under almond eyes — it was clear especially to Guy Sterling.

"I don't see anything," Dominica finally said, still frowning. "What is it?"

Guy's slight laugh suggested that life was all in all a joke and he its fool. "Looks to me," he said wryly, "like good old Canadian dirt, the kind I'd find in my own back yard." He went on, now talking to no one in particular except maybe the ultimate jokester. "We travel a hundred and fifty million miles to the Trivium Charontis and what do we come back with?" He paused, then almost snorted: "A rock garden. The whole damn mission's been a waste of time."

Dominica was now looking up. Her "Oh?" was both all innocence and all knowing.

"I mean professionally," Guy said quickly. "Personally, it's been — interesting."

Their two mouths, close together as they bent over the microscope, now touched tentatively, then more urgently.

It was a minute later before Dominica had moved away. She looked down thoughtfully, as if the shape of her nails needed serious consideration. Guy watched her.

"Problem?" Guy said at last.

"No." Dominica wasn't looking at him. "It's just that we land in a few days. It will be a matter of . . ." — she slowly raised her eyes to meet his — ". . . of adjustment." She wore a slight smile. "You *do* have a wife."

"Dominica . . ."

"It's all right." Her voice was now a wound. "We both knew what we were doing. And nothing is ever permanent, is it?"

"No . . . I suppose not." Guy rose, crossed over to her. "One thing . . ."

"Yes?"

"As you said . . ." If Dominica's words had been a challenge that Guy had failed to meet, it was now that she withdrew that challenge. Guy said simply, "We still have a few days," and they were kissing again, Dominica's body responding as his hands travelled slowly, surely, along it.

BUZZZZZ!

"Christ," Guy swore under his breath as the two lovers jumped apart. He sighed, then spoke louder, irritation in his voice as he addressed the interloper: "Yes?"

The man Steiner came through the suspended plastic sheeting that surrounded the space lab. He wore his assurance as snugly as his close-fitting tunic. Tall, and haughty, he looked at people as though he were even taller. Anyone familiar with mountaineering would have recognized his face from pictures of the much-publicized East German ascent of the Matterhorn. Others would recall the face from his later exploits at the Winter Olympics in Zurich, where he took the gold in the men's downhill.

"Excuse me," Steiner said, his smile meant to tell them he shared their little secret and enjoyed it. "Was I interrupting something?"

"If we said yes," Dominica snapped, "would you leave?"

"I simply thought you'd both be interested

to learn that we have successfully corrected course."

Guy's voice was flat: "We've heard." It was Steiner's most hateful self, the one that spoke as if on the side of the angels.

"So," Steiner said to both of them, "the mission is almost over." Then he spoke only to Dominica, his words like little sharp pokes and stabs. "Sad in a way. Now that we're almost home I won't have you to look at each morning."

Steiner had taken a step towards her and now was moving his arms around her waist.

"I doubt," Dominica said coolly as she stepped out of Steiner's way, "that will be a significant tragedy in your life, Major."

Steiner was now speaking to Guy. "It will be tragic for some, though. Partings can be difficult." He stood still for a moment, looking from one to the other. "Well," he said as he started for the door, "I'll leave you to your . . . work." Suddenly he paused, glanced round. He spoke this time with some greater disgust that was maybe the real man; he spoke quickly, almost angrily, "How can you two spend so much time in here? So many dangerous chemicals. Most depressing."

"Are you finished?" Guy snapped.

Steiner all at once composed himself; the smooth-surfaced eyes, the knowing smile, were back. "Patience, my friend. Another few days and you and I will be happily rid of one another."

Steiner nodded briefly and was gone.

Braddock walked down the passageway in his usual brisk, heel-clicking manner. The passageway gleamed with rose-coloured light, which softened the appearance of the corrugated metal walls of the space vehicle. As space crafts went, Conestoga was a big one, and the walk from the Command Deck to his cabin and back again was more than a hop, skip and jump. It was not a romp in the woods with a good retriever either, but it was far better than the cramped capsules he had jockeyed in his younger days. Conestoga would do, he thought; it almost felt like home.

Braddock suddenly stopped, hesitating before the partially open door. With a sudden intake of breath, he moved quickly again, through the door and into his cabin.

"See anything interesting, Colonel?" Braddock asked.

It was Kalsinov, the Russian cosmonaut, interrupted from looking through the papers on Braddock's desk. "Excuse me," Kalsinov tried to sound official. "I was waiting to speak to you privately."

"While you look over my personal papers?" Braddock spoke without emotion.

"Captain, as you know I am a plain man, so I will speak plainly. Neither Olga Denerenko nor I have any intention of validating your leadership of this mission."

Again, Braddock's voice gave away nothing, "That's your privilege."

"More than my privilege, it's my duty. I believe — and I will say so publicly — that your judgment has been questionable on far too many occasions."

"I'm sure you have a list."

"As it happens, I do. Your most critical error is one that we may not survive."

"Oh?" asked Braddock, as if mildly curious about the answer.

A blush crept slowly across Kalsinov's chiselled features. He was more used to having the advantage than having to fight for it. "You unnecessarily wasted fuel on the Delta 216 during liftoff from the Martian surface. I am seriously concerned that we may not have enough fuel for our re-entry."

"We've been over this."

"Not to my satisfaction," Kalsinov scolded. "I tell you frankly that if I could have mustered the support I would have assumed command of this mission many weeks ago."

Braddock now spoke in exasperation. "You take orders from your government, Colonel. It's the only way you know how to operate. You don't do things on your own." He spoke as if fed up with having always to point out the obvious.

Kalsinov stiffened, his shoulders thrust back, "Don't misjudge me, Captain."

Braddock's eyes suddenly turned cold, his voice hard, as he took several steps toward the Russian. "And don't *you* misjudge *me*. As long as we're aboard this ship I am judge, jury and executioner — and I will consider any attempt to subvert this mission an act of mutiny."

Kalsinov hesitated only for an instant before turning on his heels and striding out. Braddock's face was still grim as he glanced down at the papers on his desk. Then, just as quickly, he too left the cabin.

CHAPTER FIVE

Olga Denerenko — Russian scientist attached to the space lab project, wife of Commissar Giorgi Denerenko, himself newly appointed to the Russian Politburo by the Premier's command — sat alone and naked in her cabin, combing her long grey-blonde hair, still wet from the shower, idly running her free hand up and down her neck.

"Olga." She recognized Braddock's voice at her door.

"Come in," Olga answered. "It's not locked."

Olga Denerenko knew exactly how beautiful, how desirable, she was.

The door slid open, and there he was, Olga already laughing at his look of surprise. She laughed again and said nothing as she slowly put the comb down on the utility table, and reached just as slowly for the hair-blower beside it. Still silent, with one hand she lifted the blower to her hair while with the other she caught her hair in a tangled mass.

"Did I startle you?" she finally asked as she tilted her head to one side, moving fingers through blowing locks.

Braddock cleared his throat, still in shock, his anger just beginning. "Somewhat," he said, tight-lipped.

"Really?" She was smiling with her lips, laughing at him with her eyes. "And I thought you had such a good memory."

For a moment a look passed between them, hers daring him to remember, his willing her to live only in the present and in the roles life had assigned them. "I'd better come back," Braddock said, moving to the door uncomfortably, as if against a stiff wind.

Olga spoke like a cat mewing, "If my body now offends you, Neal, I'll cover it." It was the robe that she lifted from the bed, stood up to put on, languorously tied closed with a sash — it was the robe Braddock kept his gaze fixed on now.

Olga stretched as she asked him, "Will that do?"

Braddock's face suddenly softened, he spoke in a whisper that surprised him: "I was hoping we could talk."

"Of course you were," Olga rushed in, speaking quickly and lightly now, as if tripping down a garden path on slippered feet. "You've spoken with Kalsinov and now you want *me* to talk to him." She laughed. "Or am I mistaken?"

Braddock suddenly took a step towards her, his arm went out as if both instructing and pleading. "Look, if he goes public with his complaints he'll blow the image of this entire mission. The people want heroes," he said. "Give them a success — even if it's an illusion — and we can generate enough funds to —"

Olga's "Stop it!" startled him. "What?" Braddock asked, almost as if awakened suddenly from sleep, and Olga looked at him for a moment, remembering that it was Braddock's earnestness, his belief in whatever cause, that made her want him — to share in it with him? to break it down? She didn't know. As she dreamed for just a minute she also remembered how it was that same earnestness that allowed him to reject her.

Olga spoke now like a cat whines: "You never had a sense of irony, Neal, but it should occur to even you that you're the last person I would help." Her voice was hard, meant to set her apart from the pitiable. "Particularly since you ignored me when I needed *you*."

"Dammit, Olga, you're married . . ."

"A fact that has not discouraged others." Braddock sighed, remembering, he and Olga would always be logics apart. Olga was going on. "That is, until my husband was elevated to the Politburo . . ." She turned off the hair-blower suddenly, and put it down hard on the utility table. Her fingers were moving restlessly, twisting the sash on her robe around and around. She turned away as she spoke; her tears were not for Braddock but for herself and the bitter years. "You're all so afraid . . ."

"Regardless of what you may think of me," — Braddock seemed to stand at attention — "of this mission —"

"It's not the mission that concerns you!" Olga shouted, a cold hard voice that had heard it all before, "it's your career. That's all that's ever been important in your life, even in the beginning." She rose abruptly, grabbing up the damp towel on her bed. "Now please leave me alone. I want to remove this robe," — she glared at him — "and I'm sure it will embarrass you."

Braddock stopped outside the door of her cabin for a minute. She was crying, sobbing, the sound smothered by a damp towel, a robe.

CHAPTER SIX

Inside the Communications Center of Mission Control night was more a state of mind than a provable fact. Nowhere did daylight or moonlight have access to the busy chamber with its throbbing panels of lights and instruments. The green glow of the communications consoles gave a gloomy cast to the figures seated before them, and the group gathered in front of the giant TV screen looked like sculpture groupings until someone shifted his weight. McCallister, Carlino and other Mission Control personnel watched the familiar face of Dr Philippe Berdoux on the screen. Even enlarged, the face of the French medical officer of the mission gave no answers. He could have the blood of Talleyrand in his veins, thought McCallister as he watched Jeffrey Kilbride ponder his next question for the doctor. Kilbride was seated at a console in front of the screen. TV cameras mounted on silent pedestals moved in and out as the interview continued. Kilbride shifted pages of script in his hand. "Then, Dr Berdoux," he said, "everyone aboard seems to be in good health?"

"Oh, yes," the medical officer said, pulling at his earlobe, "except for what you Americans call the cabin fever." Berdoux spread his hands in a Gallic gesture. "Crowded together for five months — it is a situation in which relationships can be sorely tested." Berdoux smiled a smile as old as civilization. Kilbride, ever the newsman, pushed closer.

"And have they been?"

Berdoux was at once on his guard. He smiled again and shrugged disarmingly. "I was merely using a figure of speech. We are all getting along quite well."

The interviewer abandoned his line of questioning. He glanced up at the giant screen, and for a moment, as Berdoux looked at the camera in the Space Lab, there was the illusion that Kilbride and the doctor had exchanged a look. "One more medical question, Doctor. Before the mission began there was the fear that all of you might be in danger of contracting some sort of 'space disease.'" It wasn't in fact a question, but Berdoux saw what Kilbride was getting at.

"I would not concern myself with Martian

Plague," he said, enjoying the sensation his use of this highly-charged phrase would have among English-speakers on earth. "In any event, we will be undergoing extensive physical examinations in quarantine before mingling among you." His eyes twinkled as he imagined mingling again on solid earth.

"Given the limited activities aboard, Doctor, is everyone following to the prescribed exercise program?" The face on the screen broke into a broad smile. The Frenchman's eyes danced as he replied to the reporter.

"I have a confession, Mr Kilbride. One among us has been negligent." McCallister felt Carlino's body stiffen slightly at his side, as Berdoux continued. "I am embarrassed to tell you it is me. The food here is remarkably good, and being French I'm very much afraid that I have indulged myself." Kilbride smiled, and so did most of the others in the Communications Center; Braddock noticed several people sharing a grin.

"Ladies and gentlemen, this is the first time in the history of space travel someone has actually said something flattering about the food." Even Carlino joined in to share the laugh. Kilbride on his part looked like he was getting ready to wind up his examination of the witness. His next question proved it. "Is there anything else you'd like to tell us, Doctor?"

"Just that we are all well and there has not been even so much as a cold among us."

"Dr Berdoux, this interview will be broadcast

around the world. Is there anything you would like to say to your wife and friends?" Berdoux smiled, now that the hard questions were finished. He tried to imagine the face of Sabine, his wife.

"Just that I love her," he said.

McCallister and Carlino stood with others in the rear. Carlino's attention wandered from the interview to the Director. He looked at the circles under his eyes and other landmarks of severe stress. He leaned over to McCallister and whispered, "Why don't you go home and get some sleep?" McCallister, who had been close to nodding off on his feet, felt the suggestion dig into him.

"What and damage my health?" he said. "My body's not used to it."

"How's Jill, by the way? Shouldn't you be a grandfather by now?"

"She's like this mission, Mitch: long overdue." McCallister felt guilty for a second. He hadn't spared Jill a thought for several hours. Selfish bastard, he branded himself.

One of Carlino's aides was moving through the Communications Center regulars towards his boss. Carlino saw him coming and grabbed him by the arm as the aide quickly whispered something in his ear. Carlino nodded, then turned to McCallister. "We may have a problem," he said. McCallister searched Carlino's face for the rest of the answer. Carlino was looking straight ahead of him at the backs of the TV crew. He continued.

"Braddock wants to talk to you on the off-line scrambler frequency."

That jolted the Director. "What the hell's this all about? That system's only to be used in an emergency."

"Or when Braddock's got something to say he doesn't want the world to hear." McCallister's face flinched as a muscle in his cheek shortened involuntarily.

"Come on," he said. And they left the room as quietly as they could.

Mitch Carlino closed the door of McCallister's office behind him. The Director had already moved to the TV set and turned it on. Carlino watched as his chief opened a metal box atop the set to reveal an encoding panel. The picture on the screen was a swirling mass of unwatchable lines. McCallister began setting the unscrambling formula. "Four-six-uh . . ."

"Seven-one. As of two hours ago," Carlino added with as much tact as he could muster. Realizing that McCallister had a lot on his mind, he hoped that he hadn't got to the point where uninvited help was a criticism. His chief gave him a mechanical grin of thanks as he completed the setting of switches. When he stood back from the TV screen, Carlino could see a clear picture of Braddock in his cabin aboard the Space Lab. McCallister turned a switch, and the two floodlights on his flanks were also activated. On the screen, Carlino saw a flash of recognition as McCallister's face appeared on Braddock's screen.

"Neal?" tested McCallister.

"You're coming in loud and clear, Andy." All three faces relaxed. At least technology was giving the mission full support. In the Space Lab, Braddock wondered whether McCallister's face was looking older.

"What's the problem?" the Director asked, getting right down to business. Braddock liked that, and began making his report.

"The Russians," he said. "We may have a P.R. disaster on our hands. I think Olga and Colonel Kalsinov are going to denounce the mission." Braddock noticed that the Director looked off-screen towards someone. That would be Mitch Carlino, he thought.

"What the hell are you talking about?" McCallister said, leaning towards the camera.

"It's likely Kalsinov will try to discredit me. Olga will probably back him up."

"What do you mean, discredit you?"

"He's got some sort of laundry list — charges that I screwed up. And he's fixated on the shortfall of fuel for re-entry. Claims I used more than I needed." McCallister wondered whether the captain was going paranoid up there.

"Any truth to that?"

"Some," Braddock said with a tough grin. "Look, Andy, nobody calls them right all the time. I've made mistakes, but I've done a good job up here."

So, the Director mused, it's developing in a political way up there. "Who's on your side?"

"It's a six to two split. Us against the Russians."

"Six and two are eight, Neal."

"Kurt Steiner is strictly in the middle. Despises us all equally." Braddock watched McCallister soak in the effect of this news. McCallister was a good politician, but his face was as expressive as an actor's when he allowed it to be. When he had arrived at a course of action, he smiled at Braddock through the miles.

"All right, Neal, nothing much we can do at this point, but stay on top of it. And keep me informed."

"Check," said Braddock. "Talk to you soon. Over."

For a moment after Braddock's face disappeared, McCallister didn't move. It seemed like a full minute to Carlino, who was waiting for some word from his chief. McCallister frowned as he got up and turned off the TV set. It wasn't hard for Carlino to discover that he wasn't at all happy about what he'd heard.

A figure was asleep in the large bed. Dimly lit by the first traces of dawn, the figure moved under the covers as though even in sleep, the Director's responsibilities operated. Outside the window, daybreak was casting light on the eastern horizon as the neighbourhood of comfortable traditional houses slept. McCallister slept on the far edge of the bed. The covers over half the bed were undisturbed. The dry singing of crickets was

interrupted by the phone. McCallister buried his
face away from the insistent ring. He tossed fit-
fully. The phone rang a second time. "Grace,"
he muttered in a voice still heavy with sleep,
"for Christ's sake, get the phone." He reached
out over the unslept-in side of the bed and began
to prod. As the phone rang again, he sat up with
a start, knowing that his wife was not there, and
remembering why.

"Jesus!" He clambered across the king-sized
bed to his wife's empty side and groped for his
glasses and then grabbed the phone. He even managed to bring the receiver to his ear. "Hello," he
growled. It was his wife. "Grace? No, you didn't
wake me. I just got home."

He half-sat up in the bed, plumping a pillow
behind his head, and then lighting a cigarette.
He was fully awake now. "Okay, so what is it?"
He paused, then corrected the ambiguity. "I
mean, which is it? A boy or girl?" His wife spoke
at the other end of the line for some seconds.
McCallister held the receiver a little away from
his ear. He knew his wife's voice well. Its pene-
tration potential could not be measured scientif-
ically. "Grace," he interrupted, "you called me
at five-thirty to tell me nothing's happened yet."
He suddenly began to feel like a cross old bear
whose hibernation had been interrupted. He took
a drag on the cigarette and in a softer tone said,
"No, I'm not mad. How are you?" He held the
receiver away from his ear again. "That's good."
He nodded a few times as though Grace could

see him, and then answered his wife's question. "Oh, I'm a little tired. Look, you tell Jill, if she keeps this up much longer, you're coming home and she can have the baby by herself." On her end of the wire, Grace laughed, and was just about to speak when McCallister heard the line go dead. "What? Hello — Grace? Grace!"

The voice that he heard was not that of his wife of nearly a quarter of a century, but the almost sexless calm of an operator saying, "We have disconnected this call under a Priority One condition. Go ahead, please." And then it was Carlino's excited voice on the line. He was breathing hard as he spoke.

"Sorry to cut in, Doctor, but we've got a Class A emergency down here."

"What the hell's so important it can't wait?" McCallister rasped, already reconciled to the idea of beginning another day at dawn.

"Can't discuss it on the phone. We need you down here five minutes ago." McCallister's feet were rooting around the bedroom broadloom for yesterday's socks.

"I'll be there in twenty, Mitch," he said, and broke the connection. He went over in his mind all the possible ends that might have started unravelling, while taking a fast shower.

The press were waiting for him like zoo animals at feeding time. He parked the car and got out on the run. The camera crews of four networks tried to cut him off. Reporters pressed close, peppering him with questions. In the forefront was the inevitable Jeffrey Kilbride holding a microphone with the network logo on top.

"Dr McCallister, can you tell us what's happened?" The Director kept moving. He knew that it was fatal to stop. If he even paused, he'd be in for an impromptu press conference. He called back at Kilbride, "You know as much as I do."

"We had a two-way interview with Space Lab scheduled for eight a.m. All of a sudden they've pulled the plug. No reason given. And now the building's totally off-limits to all press."

McCallister shrugged in as friendly a manner as he could. He didn't want to alienate Kilbride, who after all had his uses. He repeated what he'd already said and added, "Can't help you, sorry."

Two armed military policemen barred the reporters from the familiar concrete and glass front of Mission Control. The Director went right through the doors that were held open for him. A couple of reporters tried to break through, but the guards firmly escorted them back through the doors.

McCallister's face brightened. He'd seen Carlino heading towards him. Good, he thought, no more suspense.

"What happened, Mitch? We lose 'em again?"

"No, Andy," Carlino said in a tight voice. "We've still got them. *Most* of them." McCallister picked this up, and flashed Carlino a look. Carlino took in his breath while he watched the face of the Director. "Olga Denerenko's dead."

"What?" McCallister was genuinely startled. This was not one of the loose ends he had anticipated.

"You heard me."

"Dead? What do you mean dead? *How* dead? People her age don't just die."

"Yeah, I know."

McCallister felt the fact gain an unwilling acceptance in his brain. "Oh, shit!" he said.

CHAPTER SEVEN

McCallister collapsed into his office chair. Distracted, it was as if he only overheard what Carlino now explained to him, "Braddock and Dr Berdoux are standing by to talk. Oh, and I contacted our Medical Officer." McCallister nodded. "She's waiting for you," Carlino added, and with a second nod from McCallister, went and opened the door to the outer office.

In another minute a tall, black woman was standing in front of McCallister's desk. "Dr McCallister," Margaret Leigh, the Medical Officer, said, and McCallister was struck by the errant thought that if she were as dedicated to her looks as to her profession, Dr Margaret Leigh would be a stunningly beautiful woman. As it was, she was just plain beautiful.

"Morning, Margaret," he said after a minute, and then after another distracted pause, he heaved himself up from his chair and moved to the TV set. While Carlino and Margaret waited, McCallister opened the scrambler box on top of the set, set the keys and flipped it on. The screen lit up, first showing a grey haze and then the images of Braddock and Berdoux.

"Neal," barked McCallister, "what the hell's going on?" He'd swung his office chair around to face the set, and now sank back into it.

Braddock spoke quickly. "Look, Andy, we're as confused as you are, but Olga's dead. Dominica Mastrelli found her in her cabin about two hours ago. Dr Berdoux figures she died," — Braddock turned to Berdoux, his shoulders hunching up — "how long ago?"

"Possibly an hour or so before her body was discovered," the Doctor answered. "No more. I can't tell you how or why, Dr McCallister. It could have been anything — stroke, heart attack, blood clot, aneurism. We won't know until we can perform an autopsy."

"Wait a minute," said McCallister. "You want us to bring her down — without knowing the cause of death? It could be anything." McCallister had turned to Margaret Leigh, who was listening but not looking at the screen. Berdoux spoke like a practical man: "I understand, but we have no choice."

"Perhaps we do," Margaret broke in, now moving to McCallister.

"What?" McCallister said.

"I said perhaps we do have a choice." She leaned towards the screen. "Can you see me?" she said to Berdoux. "It's Doctor Margaret Leigh."

"Ah, yes, Doctor." Berdoux offered a half-collegial, half-enchanted smile.

"Would it be possible," Margaret said, speaking with her usual cool intensity, "to place Mrs Denerenko's body in the pod you use for physical examinations, then hook it up to the sensors and X-ray scanner here at ground control?"

Berdoux answered in a tone that suggested he was ready to play with a curious mathematical problem. "It's possible. I don't know what you'd get."

Margaret said matter-of-factly, "A complete skeletal X-ray, chemical analysis on the blood, urine, and other body fluids." She suddenly paused, then smiled, "You'd be surprised what our computers can ferret out."

"May I remind you, Doctor," said Berdoux, "this system was developed for use on living organisms."

Margaret shrugged. "I didn't say it would be perfect, but it might give us something."

McCallister, listening intently, now looked to Berdoux: "Doc?"

Berdoux tilted his head from side to side. "Well, I suppose it's worth a try. An autopsy a half-million miles into space." He nodded to Margaret. "A novel approach, Dr Leigh."

Berdoux glanced at Braddock, who seemed

to make a decision. "We'll get back to you later, Andy," he said hurriedly. McCallister had hardly said, "Right," before shutting off the scrambler and turning to face Margaret.

"What do you think, Margaret? Will it really work?"

"We won't know till we try," she answered cheerfully.

McCallister half laughed, half snorted. "That's what I like. Certainty." He waved her away. "Go to it."

Guy Sterling and Kurt Steiner, straining under the literally dead weight, carried the sheet-wrapped body through the enveloping plastic partitions into the lab. Philippe Berdoux, Pamela and Braddock were already there, and watched as the two men, with twin grunts, heaved the body of Olga Denerenko on to a cot. Its lid raised, the clear plastic pod next to the cot sat ready as a temporary tomb.

"This procedure is degrading!" It was Kalsinov.

"Perhaps," Braddock answered matter-of-factly. "But Mission Control won't clear us to land until they can isolate the cause of Olga's death."

"And if they cannot do so?" Kalsinov sniped.

Braddock's face was expressionless as he stared at the colonel. "Let's not consider that possibility."

Kalsinov turned away sharply, almost collid-

ing with Guy and Steiner as he marched toward
the door. He stopped, bowed at the two men,
then followed them out of the room.

"I'll let you know," Berdoux now said to Braddock, "when we have something definitive."

Braddock gone, Philippe now turned to Pamela, who was standing by the cot. She glanced
at him, then down. She trembled as she began
to undrape the corpse. She stared at the naked
form. And suddenly, her hand letting go of the
sheet, she turned and crossed the room. "I don't
think I'll be much help," Pamela said in a voice
made husky by the tears she was holding back.

Berdoux had followed her, and now touched
her arm gently. "Of course you will."

"No . . ." She hesitated. "You were right about
one thing." She was trying to laugh. "I would
have made a terrible doctor."

Berdoux's voice was as gentle as his touch.
"Did I really tell you that?"

"The University of Paris. Lecture Hall B."
Pamela mimicked Berdoux's accent with mixed,
but endearing, effect: "I believe your quote was:
'Miss Cooper, you are a brilliant student em-
barking on a career for which you are emotion-
ally unsuited.'"

"I don't recall." Berdoux looked at her smiling, mock wonderment on his face. "Your memory is remarkable."

"It's not an easy thing to forget," said Pamela,
and rushed on, trying through speed to outwit
her embarrassment. "When you're twenty-two,

and you're curtly dismissed by a teacher for
whom you have a great deal of . . ." — she was
blushing, stammering — "affection . . ." She
looked at the floor, not seeing Berdoux's smile
sadden. "I don't suppose you recall that either."

He was nodding. "As a matter of fact I do,
and I was wondering how long it would take us
to bring it up. Pamela," — she looked up at the
sound of her name — "if it means anything at
this late date, you were not the only one with
feelings of affection." Berdoux was studying her
carefully, intently, pausing to see and feel the
effect on her of his words. "Had I not been married — were I not *still* married . . ."

A moment passed before Pamela, taking a deep
breath, said softly, "This isn't a very suitable
conversation. I mean, under the circumstances."

"No," Philippe Berdoux answered quietly.

Pamela tried on a chipper smile. "Then shall
we get to it? I hope I remember enough of my
pre-medical education to be of some help."

"I'm sure," Berdoux spoke gently, "I'm sure
you will."

The two worked calmly, deliberately, raising
Olga's body to a working level inside the pod,
keeping her legs together and her arms straight
and stiff against her sides. Berdoux pulled a
sensor from a panel above the pod, a needle attached by a long wire. Taking Olga's wrist, he
tried to insert the needle.

"Would you like me to try?" Pamela asked
after a moment or two, watching the doctor
fumble.

"Yes, please." Berdoux handed the sensor to Pamela, and as she quickly slipped the needle into the vein, explained: "My fingers are a little arthritic." He spoke with resignation. "The years are catching up."

Margaret Leigh was typing instructions on the computer keyboard while Carlino waited behind her. An anatomical abstract of what had been Olga Denerenko appeared on her display terminal.

"She's hooked up," Margaret said. "Let's see what we've got."

More typing. Waiting. Suddenly the machine responded. Margaret hit several more keys in rapid succession. Pause. Then it began: Body Temperature, Blood Content, Chemical Composition of Body Fluids . . .

"What's the matter?" Dominica asked Guy.

He had risen abruptly from the microscope and began pacing the room. "Nothing," he answered as he began to rub his eyes.

"No," Dominica insisted, "something is wrong."

"Look," he said, "I'm tired, that's all. In the excitement I forgot to take my insulin shot."

Dominica looked at him quizzically. "You're upset about Olga."

"For Christ sake, Dominica," Guy exploded, "she *is* dead. At least you could pretend *some* sympathy."

"I'm sorry," Dominica answered but in a voice that said she'd be damned if she would be. "You know how I felt about her. I didn't hide it."

"You sure as hell didn't."

"And what does *that* mean?"

"I don't know . . ." Guy now sounded suddenly less angry and more puzzled. "But you seemed to get an excessive amount of pleasure out of cutting her off from me."

Dominica's voice was cold, hard. "You didn't seem to object. If I recall, you were more than willing to replace her."

"I just don't like the feeling of being anyone's trophy. Hers or yours."

"Poor Guy," Dominica said wryly. "Suffering the guilt of the damned. This once don't punish yourself. You didn't use her — *she* used *you*."

"Listen, dammit!" Guy stopped speaking as he suddenly leaned forward. Dominica had grabbed him, stopping his fall.

"Guy!" she said, alarmed.

"I'm sorry," he murmured. "I've got to take my shot."

Recovering just enough energy, Guy left the room. Dominica didn't move for a minute.

CHAPTER EIGHT

At Mission Control, the day wore on. Those in the know and those whose security rating excluded special information went about their jobs. But even the maintenance engineers repairing electronic circuits and the cleaning staff were aware that something was up. That took a human brand of sensitivity that could not be licensed or revoked. In McCallister's outer office Dinah was managing the traffic.

"Mr McCallister's office."

"Jeffrey Kilbride, Dinah. Is he there?" At the moment the reporter asked, McCallister himself appeared, emerging from his office. He paused to listen."

"I'm sorry, Mr Kilbride," said Dinah, catching McCallister's eye for a second, "he's away from his desk." McCallister winked his approval of Dinah's methods of handling both media calls and the literal truth. He placed some papers for typing in front of his secretary, and returned to his own room.

At IBN News, Jeffrey Kilbride was leaning back in his swivel chair, munching a handful of Taco chips. A group of aides were screening news footage on three monitors in his busy office. Kilbride tried to turn on the charm with Dinah. "Hey, c'mon, Dinah. I've gotta speak to him. Gimme a break."

"I have you down on the sheet, sir," Dinah said in an even voice that announced between the words, "Don't try to get around me, buster!" What she actually said was, "He'll get back to you as soon as he can."

"Tell him it's urgent." After Dinah acknowledged this, Kilbride broke the connection. His hand went for the bag of chips again. After a slight hesitation he dialled another number. His impatient fingers drummed on an unread script in front of him as the call pulsed in his ear.

"This is Jeffrey Kilbride, IBN News. Put me through to Harry Devlin. He's with the Vice-President's party." Kilbride's fingers continued their drumming and the call advanced through the circuitry.

"No, damn it, no interview, no pictures." McCallister was seated at his desk with Mitch Carlino standing by. Before them on McCallister's desk was a sheaf of computer printouts, from which the insistent telephone had interrupted them. "When we have a statement to make, we'll make it." McCallister slapped the receiver back on its base. Carlino leaned closer to his chief.

"Andy, we're springing a few leaks," he said, as though he was trying to pass the news without the anxiety that went with it. "There's speculation in Paris. The French President has called the White House looking for confirmation. A reporter in Bonn's been after the Embassy . . ."

The buzzer sounded, and the Director hit the key angrily.

"Yes!" It was Dinah's voice that came on the speaker after just the slightest pause. Dinah was devoted to McCallister, but she wasn't a doormat.

"Excuse me, but Senator Carlisle's on line one and Alexander Rostov is waiting to see you."

"Stall the Senator, send in Rostov, and I'm sorry."

McCallister could read Dinah's widening smile through the wall separating them. "Of course you are," she said.

McCallister moved away from the desk as the door opened and Rostov entered, closing the door firmly behind him. Carlino examined the Russian's face. He looked ashen as he approached the desk and stared at McCallister with great sadness. Carlino's heart felt a kindred heaviness in the badly tailored chest of his opposite number. McCallister thought the Russian was on the edge of tears.

"Andrew, my friend, why was I not informed of Olga Denerenko's death?" He spoke as though he had been speaking for many hours. His voice barely covered the syllables. For once it was hard to find the politician under his disarming exterior. He had sloughed the snakeskin for the moment at least. Out of habit, Carlino tried to put him on the defensive.

"Where'd you learn that?"

Rostov looked from one face to the other out of infinite sadness. "Perhaps I have been misled?"

Carlino and McCallister exchanged glances. This was one of those moments not covered by any secret manual of conduct before the potential enemy. McCallister shifted in his chair, and motioned Rostov to a seat near him.

"No," he said, moving towards a frank disclosure. "I only wish you had been."

"And the cause of death?"

McCallister made a wide gesture. "At the moment, undetermined."

The Russian smiled sadly and repeated "undetermined", while pulling at the creases in his trousers with hairy-wristed hands. He leaned close to the desk.

"Andrew, forgive me. I have also learned you are conducting — what — an *autopsy* through space? Really, can such a thing have merit?"

McCallister pulled at his chin for a moment.

"We hope so," he said. "If there *is* some strange virus aboard the lab, and I hope to God there isn't — "

"Of course, of course," Rostov protested, waving his hands to show that all sane and civilized men think alike on such matters. "Personally, I find the notion of such an examination . . ." He searched for the word. "Distasteful. Officially, I must register my protest . . ." He shrugged off the official protest and returned to the informal manner that he had achieved in the Doctor's office. "But since you are going ahead," — he smiled up at the Director and turned his head to include Carlino in its warmth — "I trust you will give me a full and complete report of your findings."

"Naturally," said McCallister, as Carlino bristled off to the side, out of sight of the Russian.

At that moment, the intercom at McCallister's elbow buzzed. He answered more calmly than earlier. "Yes?"

"Dr Leigh is here, sir."

"Ask her to wait, Dinah." The Russian began to bluster.

"Surely not on *my* account. If Dr Leigh has the results, we are all vitally interested to learn what they are." McCallister weighed the reasonableness of the request, then got back to Dinah.

"Send her in."

The door opened and Margaret Leigh entered McCallister's office carrying a sheaf of papers and several folders. On seeing Rostov sitting next to the Director's desk, her face betrayed a scarcely detectable note of surprise, which she quickly covered with a look of involved seriousness. McCallister was the first to get to his feet as the doctor came in. The other two followed a moment after.

"Doctor," McCallister said, "you know Mr Rostov, the Soviet liaison officer?"

"We've met," answered Dr Leigh a little more formally than necessary. She tried to improve things with a smile. Meanwhile the Russian was bowing warmly over her hand which he had taken in his great paws.

"I am charmed, as always, and most anxious to learn the results of your post-mortem tests."

"I'm sorry," began Margaret Leigh, "the results were inconclusive. There's every indication Olga Denerenko died of a massive brain hemorrhage, but we won't be able to confirm that diagnosis until the body is returned to earth." The three men in the room looked at the woman before them. It was the Russian who broke the tension.

"I see," he said sarcastically, "and no hint of any strange intergalactic virus?"

Amused, or almost, the medical officer shook her head: "No." The Russian looked at McCallister.

"Then at least the mission is not in jeopardy," he said turning his head to one side with humorous effect. "I'm looking forward to a complete report of your findings, Doctor. At the moment Commissar Denerenko knows nothing of this tragedy. I feel so sorry for him. He and his young wife were very much in love."

Once more the official personage, Rostov bowed his way out of the inner office. Again the buzzer at McCallister's elbow sounded.

"Yes?"

"Sir," Dinah's voice was steady but beginning to show the tension of these last few days. "It's Harry Devlin, the Vice-President's chief assistant, on the line."

McCallister and Carlino exchanged a glance which when decoded might read something like "Here we go again." The Director picked up the phone. "Harry," he said pleasantly and he hoped disarmingly. "What can I do for you?"

A government limousine, shiny with importance, made its way through traffic. The chauffeur, in immaculate livery, was separated from the passengers by a glass panel. From time to time he looked at his passengers in the rear-view mirror: a white man from the Mission Complex and a black woman. They were talking, and he tried to imagine what he might make of their conversation if he could hear it. He liked the way the white man listened to the black woman, and treated her like a lady. The car sped through the foothills towards the city's poshest hotels. Who knows what sights he'd see when he delivered his cargo safe and sound to the hotel.

In the back seat McCallister tried to relax. The unfamiliar tug of the necktie he had put on in honour of the occasion, made him uncomfortable. He felt heavy and uncomfortable in his winter outerwear, while the woman sitting next to him seemed cosy and warm in her fur collar. Outside, the drab winter landscape scudded past them. He had thought better of lighting a cigarette. He'd try to grab one on his way to the Veep. Margaret Leigh broke the silence that had lasted for several miles. "Okay, Doctor," she said. "You can forget what I said in front of Rostov." McCallister cocked his head and looked at his company from a new angle.

"And I thought *I* was the only political animal in this car." He laughed and she joined him. Dr Leigh took some stapled papers from an envelope and handed it to McCallister.

"Here's what *really* happened to Olga Denerenko."

McCallister returned the papers as the car bumped over a level crossing. "Just give it to me in three sentences or less."

Margaret's face lit up with the stimulation of the problem the Director had posed. A concise report. Very well, he shall have one. "One," she said aloud, "there was a heavy concentration of barbiturates in her system. Not enough to kill her, but enough to knock her out. Two, the most probable cause of death is asphyxiation, but I couldn't prove it. And — "

"Wait a minute. What are you saying? That

she was *murdered?*" McCallister looked at Margaret sitting calmly next to him talking about murder, a murder in space.

"It's highly probable."

"Jesus!" Dr Leigh looked at McCallister working on this information. She knew that that was not the end of it. She hadn't told him her third point yet.

"I'm afraid, sir, that's not the worst of it."

McCallister looked at her in disbelief.

The Vice-President, too, had a look of disbelief on his face when the Director of the International Space Exploration Administration told him the news. If McCallister was any judge, he would guess that the Veep's disbelief was total.

"Pregnant? The woman was pregnant?"

McCallister and Dr Leigh both nodded. "Yes, Mr Vice-President," said McCallister. "About two months into term." The Veep caught Margaret with his dark eyes reaching out from under heavy eyebrows.

"You're sure about this, young lady?"

"Yes, sir." The Veep frowned and banged his fist on the antique desk that was the centrepiece in the calculated elegance of the hotel suite.

"Well," he said at length. "It's a mess isn't it? *Five* months in space, *two* months pregnant." He rolled his eyes towards the restored Italian ceiling. "And," he added in another register, "you don't know for sure how she died?"

"Someone either strangled or smothered her," Margaret said simply, as if she were giving advice to a slightly dim graduate student.

"You know you're talking murder." Margaret looked back at the Veep and answered smoothly, "You asked me a medical question, sir. I gave you a medical answer."

A cat can look at a queen, McCallister thought, and moved in. "Sir, the immediate problem is that we can't keep her death a secret forever. The longer we delay, the more it's going to smell." McCallister wished to withdraw his last phrase once it was out. It was too melodramatic, and also made him think of the poor dead girl in the Conestoga Space Lab.

The Veep paused and then asked, "What do you suggest?"

McCallister's tongue moistened his lips. "We announce her untimely death due to causes unknown. The news people will go crazy no matter what we say, but maybe we can reduce the speculation." The Vice-President gathered his lower lip into a V between his thumb and forefinger as he thought it through.

"All right," he said, "but nothing about the pregnancy. Not until I confer with the President."

"Yes, sir," McCallister said. The Veep looked from McCallister to Dr Leigh and back again, soberly.

"It seems we have a murderer aboard that space lab," he said. "Forgetting everything else, the political ramifications are appalling." The Vice-President reached for his pipe on a small Louis Quinze sidetable, and began packing in loose tobacco with his knuckle. After a moment he looked up at Andrew McCallister through those much-caricatured eyebrows and said, "Andy, I'm damned if I have any advice . . ." He fixed McCallister with his striking dark eyes. The Director felt like he was on the point of a sword. ". . . but Andy, handle it."

McCallister heard himself say, "Yes, sir."

CHAPTER NINE

The comfortable but hardly palatial house of Giorgi Denerenko lay well beyond Red Square and the Kremlin on the outskirts of the capital. The house was modestly impressive in the Eastern way, with a high fence and two black unmarked cars parked near the entrance. In the shadows, four topcoated figures tried to keep their surveillance out of sight. An armed guard stood outside the front door. The night was heavy with fog rolling up from the river. Occasionally a cough could be heard from the depths of the shadows.

The livingroom was full of Cuban cigar smoke. Brandy glasses were lifted in honour of the amiable host. The light in the room was golden, and well suited the laughter that filled the room. "No, no, no, Constantine," Denerenko said, laughing and waving his cigar expansively. "These English — they live on past glories. Flag, King and Empire. But who runs the country? Shopkeepers! And I've always found men of trade to be realists. They come around, believe me."

Giorgi Denerenko was a tall and lean man in his late sixties. He looked like an aging film actor who had played leading men in hundreds of films of the 1940s. His ready smile, his enemies said, showed sharp teeth. Denerenko's three friends leaned toward the speaker as he talked. Although he had known each of them for many years, he had never before entertained them as a member of the esteemed Politburo. As he enlarged on his subject of the British as predictable tradesmen, an aide entered the room on silent feet and quietly whispered to his chief. Denerenko nodded at once and rose from the sofa.

"But Giorgi," said one of the friends.

"You will excuse me," he said, giving a smile that opened the hospitality of the house to his guests. "An urgent call from the Kremlin." Then he added, thinking that perhaps already he was beginning to sound stuffy, even among his old comrades, "From the Kremlin what other kind is there?" He picked up the telephone on a Louis Quatorze sideboard with an ormolu clock facing the company. "Yes, this is Giorgi Denerenko." The Russian smiled as he recognized a friendly voice at the other end of the line. "Ah, Peter, my friend, what is this urgent news that drags me from my guests?" He shared a smile with the guests, who seemed to be enjoying their proximity to the corridors of power. As the expression on Denerenko's face changed, his friends looked from his face to one another. They could see the effect of the Kremlin news as his features went ashen. "There must be some mistake." This was a vain protest against the truth, and it sounded like it. Denerenko's shoulders drooped as he began to accept the impossible information about his young wife's death aboard Conestoga. "I see," he said, without seeing. "Yes, yes, thank you," he said impatiently. The details could wait. He could barely take it in as it was. "Yes, I shall be here."

Old comrades watched a perceptibly older man hang up the telephone. He had forgotten that they were sitting in the living room with him. The cigars and brandy appeared to have vanished with the sound of the telephone receiver being replaced. Denerenko hesitated for a minute, with his eyes fixed on nothing in particular, then he turned to his aide. "Contact Mission Control," he said grimly. "I must speak to Alexander Rostov immediately."

CHAPTER TEN

Irene Tremayne's rented car sped along the familiar stretch of road between Mission Control and her hotel. It had almost become a second home, she thought, and the idea depressed her. The usual pattern of fast-food outlets moved by her at fifty-five miles an hour without Mrs Tremayne noticing very much. In her rear-view mirror she could see the silhouette of the gantry getting smaller. She knew that it wouldn't disappear. She had been up and down that short ten-mile straight run so many times that it haunted her dreams. She remembered driving David, the navigator aboard Conestoga, from the hotel to Mission Control. She remembered their partings. There had been several of them, as the mission waited for weather conditions to improve. In the end, David had caught a ride with Guy Sterling, the young Canadian aboard the same mission.

Irene Tremayne had often been told that she resembled the former Jacqueline Kennedy. Her dark hair hung in unequal thick ramparts on either side of an expressive face. Her coat came from a name designer and it was fairly new.

She pulled off the highway and drove toward the familiar cut-stone facade. Someday, she thought, somebody would write down the truth about what it was like to be an astronaut's wife. As she parked her car in the lot, she suddenly became aware of the hordes of media types running to her side of the car. Cameras were flashing, and floodlights raised even before the car had come to a full stop. She could hardly get the door open. The lights made all the faces meld into one face, all except for the ubiquitous Jeffrey Kilbride, who had been on her tail for a long time. Irene bit hard, and shouldered her way from the car to the front door.

"Mrs Tremayne," Kilbride asked loudly, "have you been informed of the death of Olga Denerenko?" Before she could answer, or even say "no comment," a woman reporter with a professionally hard face moved in.

"Do you feel your husband David's in any personal danger?" asked the redheaded woman with a small compact tape recorder.

"No, why should he be?" Irene tried to make

her way through the gauntlet of the working press.

"We've heard reports there may be some dead-ly virus aboard the spacecraft . . ."

"I haven't heard that." She tried to push her way through the reporters. The cameras and tape recorders parted only reluctantly. "Would you get out of my way, please?"

The redheaded reporter with the tape re-corder pursued her to the hotel door. "If David were here now, what would you say to him?" Irene stumbled, finding it difficult to close the door on at least six outstretched microphones. Through the heavy door she heard Kilbride, still not giving up.

"Mrs Tremayne, I'd like to come in and tape a short interview, if you don't mind." Irene Tre-mayne tried to control her temper, but she found that it was beyond her power.

"I do mind. Please, just leave me *alone!*"

Reaching her room, she slipped the bolt of the lock and leaned for a moment with her back against the closed door. She breathed a sigh of relief. She was thinking of taking a good long soak in the tub before dealing with anything further. The Conestoga could move much closer to the earth in the time it took her to soak off the day's frustrations in a hot bath.

She threw her coat on the bed and began to un-fasten her blouse, but her fingers stopped at the third button. They went to the radio and turned it on. She'd become a news junky, she thought. She had to face that. While the radio warmed up, she went to the closet and brought back a brand-name suitcase and put it on the bed.

On the radio one of those ersatz network scientists who are always dishing up instant theories to fit any occasion was trying to sound sage and reasonable.

"Frankly, Tom, I don't think we can rule out radioactivity as the cause of the woman's death. Our first-hand knowledge of the Martian surface is almost minimal and because we were out of contact with the returning space lab for so many weeks, we haven't yet had a chance to get a full run-down on the discoveries that may have been made."

Irene opened the suitcase and took an envelope which was lying on top, and looked at it. In her hands it was clear that this was not an unopened letter, but one that she had read several times. The voice of the interviewer interrupted her thinking.

"In other words, you're suggesting that the Martian surface could be highly radioactive — in which case *all* members of the Conestoga Space Lab team may have been affected."

"I'm suggesting nothing," the deep voice of reason intoned ponderously, "I'm merely proposing a possible hypothesis to explain the Russian woman's untimely death."

Irene slowly took the letter from the envelope, and was on the point of rereading it, when there was a knock at the door. She started, thinking about the media boys and girls on the prowl again. She called out: "Who is it?"

"Irene, it's Eleanor Sterling." The voice of a friend. Guy, David, Eleanor and herself were all in the same boat, or nearly the same boat. Quickly, Irene slipped the letter back into the suitcase, and replaced the suitcase in the closet. She turned off the radio on her way to the door.

Eleanor Sterling was a mousy little thing in her early thirties. She was at least seven months pregnant, and had not yet found the glow that writers on the subject claim is the reward for this promising condition. Irene looked past her visitor as she opened the door. "Well, I see we got rid of the press." Irene sounded stronger to herself than she felt inside. There was something about the drab Canadian hausfrau that brought out the best in Irene. Irene watched as her guest walked into the room trembling.

"I heard it — on the way from the airport. Oh, God, Irene, it's awful." Irene sat Eleanor down on the edge of the bed and took her stubby neglected fingers in her own well-manicured ones.

"Eleanor," she said, trying to comfort the girl. "We don't know enough yet. We need more information." It was clear that Eleanor was on the brink of a breakdown. Irene thought that they were all in the same condition. Some showed it more, that was all.

"But how did Olga die? The terrible things they're saying on the radio — disease, radioactivity . . ."

"They don't know what they're talking about." She said it so that she almost believed it herself.

Eleanor's eyes fell to her enlarged belly, then looked directly into Irene's eyes.

"I left the kids in Toronto with my mother," she said with evident pain. "If anything happened to Guy — I . . ."

Irene took Eleanor in her arms and held her. Soon great sobs wracked the woman's body. Irene heard herself say, quietly, as though to a child, "There, there; there, there."

CHAPTER ELEVEN

Philippe Berdoux, bent over the open pod, was no longer watching the indicator panel from which needles and probes extended to the body of Olga Denerenko. His hands resting on the edge of the pod, his head hanging down, he tried to focus on the body itself, which seemed in his confused vision to float now in the air, its outline slowly changing shape. Not a body but some indistinguishable fleshy mass floating on top of an ever-moving sea. Berdoux groaned, shook his head, then pressed one hand, hard, against his temple.

"Philippe?" Pamela Cooper was suddenly by his side. "Philippe? Are you all right?"

Berdoux, turning, both arms now stretched out

in front of him as if preparing for a fall, seemed to grope in the air for something to steady himself. With Pamela holding his arm, leading him to one side of the cabin, he at last sat slowly down.

"Just a headache," Berdoux said weakly, trying to smile. "It's nothing."

"Nothing?" Pamela spoke quietly, but there was alarm in her voice. Berdoux was trying now to get up, one arm waving her away, but she gently, both hands on his shoulders, pushed him down. "Sit down," she said, "I want to take a look at you."

Berdoux had leaned back and closed his eyes, as Pamela began to search through his medical bag. At the sounds she was making, he opened one eye. "No," he murmured. "I have to re-examine Olga." His struggle to get up was ineffective, leaving him looking like an infant, arms and legs waving in its crib. "Mission Control has evaluated the test results," he went on. "They've asked for a visual scan of the body."

Pamela had retrieved the opthalmoscope and was bending over him. "I said *sit*. Now, look up into the light."

Berdoux seemed suddenly to find his strength, grasping the hand in which she held the instrument and looking hard into Pamela's face. "No," he said sharply. There was a pause, the two of them frozen together as if in combat, then Berdoux's hand relaxed, his body slid back in the chair. "You needn't look," he said, in a voice

tired of the pretence, angered by the truth. "I'll
tell you what's wrong." He waited another moment, turning away while Pamela seemed to
study him intently. "It's a subcutaneous growth.
Possibly a tumour."

Pamela winced, then sounded a choked sob.

"Please, my dear," Berdoux said gently, pat-
ting her arm. "I am not dead nor do I intend
to be." He was all a kind, gently teasing, father
now.

Pamela, still holding back tears, said, "It can't
be a tumour. They'd never have let you on this
mission." She spoke urgently, as if she could
force him to agree, to say it wasn't so.

A minute passed, then: "I suspected it only
a few weeks before we launched." Pamela was
still staring, not wanting to hear. "I was able to
falsify my final X-rays. It's probably benign. In
any case, I'm certain it's operable and it will be
attended to as soon as we return to Earth."

"Philippe . . . I —"

He interrupted her; he spoke firmly, as one
who commands with a light touch but commands
nevertheless. "Meanwhile, I have an examination to perform, and I will be most grateful
for your help."

Pamela paused. She knew that Philippe had
quietly but firmly closed the door on the subject
of his own condition. Whether she could open it
again to any useful purpose remained to be seen.
"Is there anything specific they want us to look
for?" she asked in the voice of the dutiful assistant.

Berdoux answered straightforwardly: "Evidence of strangulation."

He would not look at Pamela's startled expression, at the questions it asked.

On the Command Deck, Dominica and David Tremayne were working busily, silently, feeding the necessary information into the main computer console, following the instructions it returned. Aware only of the lit screen, the faint whirr, neither heard Kurt Steiner come in — it was only when Dominica felt him at her back that she stiffened. Steiner, the smile on his face showing that he enjoyed her discomfort, moved closer and bent over her shoulder. His lips touched the tip of her soft pink ear. "What help can I give you?" he murmured, laughing softly.

"Please," Dominica said, her voice half angry, half full of disgust. "We're trying to work."

David's eyes never left the screen, but he spoke to Steiner in a hard voice, its meaning clear. "You were useful climbing in and out of Martian craters. Right now you're not needed. Understand?" He spoke the last as a threat, but Steiner only laughed.

Still speaking to Dominica, Steiner's voice was full of mock surprise. "I believe he's actually trying to intimidate me."

At that moment Kalsinov entered. He strode over quickly to the East German, glaring at him. "Major Steiner," he ordered, "get off the deck."

Steiner only shrugged, but had stepped back at the sound of Kalsinov's voice. He kept his answer light, easy. "You are offended, Comrade," he said, as if the fact were curious. "And are we to be in a constant state of mourning until we land?"

Kalsinov moved toward Steiner. "You *will* show Olga Denerenko respect." And Steiner, with a small tight smile and a slight bow, said, "Of course, Colonel. My apologies."

Steiner made to leave, just as Guy Sterling walked in, from the pink-lighted passageway. Kalsinov asked no one in particular, meaning everyone to pay attention, "Where is Miss Cooper?"

It was Guy who answered, nodding, "The medical lab. She's helping Doctor Berdoux re-examine the body."

Kalsinov's cool authority now crumbled before his alarm and fury, as he turned and ran from the Command Deck.

Back in the lab, Pamela and Berdoux were now working with the corpse. Berdoux felt along the backs of its heels and calves. Holding a small, high-powered light and mirror to its face, Pamela peered into Olga's nasal passages. She frowned, looked closer. Another minute and she reached for a pair of forceps, which she then used, carefully, extracting something from one of the nostrils.

Just then, the door flew open and Kalsinov stormed through it. "You will stop this immediately," he shouted, but Pamela proceeded at her slow, careful pace. Placing the microscopic fragment in a small round glass disc, she answered without looking at Kalsinov, without taking her eye off the forceps and disc. "We have orders from Mission Control." Berdoux had neither looked at Kalsinov, nor spoken.

"I do not take orders from them, Miss Cooper," Kalsinov shouted even more angrily. He moved towards her. "And you will not desecrate this woman's body."

Pamela spoke firmly, as if to an unreasonable child. "No disrespect is intended, but this examination must be conducted. If you have a problem, I suggest you take it up with Captain Braddock." She returned, with the light and mirror, to her examination, now of the mouth cavity.

"I am no longer interested in taking matters up with Captain Braddock," Kalsinov said, slamming shut the lid of the plastic pod and turning to glare at both Pamela and Berdoux. "I warn you both. Leave her alone."

Kalsinov stormed out of the room as angrily as he'd stormed in.

"Bloody asshole," Pamela muttered to Berdoux. Then one eyebrow shot up. "You'd think he had something to hide."

CHAPTER TWELVE

Night in the Communications Center at the International Space Exploration Administration was something you took on faith. There were no windows looking out to the sky from the nerve centre of Mission Control. ISEA's contact with the universe was essentially electronic, and when the huge TV was activated so that it seemed to take the earthbound viewers to the command deck of the Conestoga Space Lab without effort, it was easy to forget the bright star-dotted canopy of the sky that covered the whole complex, visible only from the executive offices.

The figures on the TV screen at the moment were those of Captain Neal Braddock and Kurt Steiner. They were talking via a network-space hook-up to Jeffrey Kilbride, whose familiar silhouette was dwarfed by the giant figures on the screen in front of him.

"I feel a deep sense of loss," Braddock was saying, "which I know is shared by the others."

"Speaking for myself," Steiner put in, "I can say only that Olga Denerenko was a great scientist and a great humanitarian. I shall miss her very much." Steiner looked grim and sallow in the uncertain colour of the TV reception.

"Bullshit," whispered McCallister under his breath. He didn't believe any of them. He was standing next to a computer console at the rear of the room. He listened to the crew members expressing their sense of shock and loss at the death of their companion in space without being taken in by their conventional phrases. He'd like to tear a strip off the lot of them and then they'd be able to hear something worth listening to. McCallister was thinking about this when his portable paging device began to whimper its beep-beep-beep sound on his belt. The Director looked down and saw the flashing red light. He turned off the sound and silently left the chamber.

Assembled in his inner office, McCallister found Mitch Carlino with Margaret Leigh. They sat facing Alexander Rostov, who rose, like a host, when McCallister came in.

"Andrew," he said, "I am sorry to take you from the press conference."

"It's all pretty predictable." Rostov smiled at the Director's candour, and hoped that it would lead to further frankness.

"Commissar Denerenko has been informed of his wife's passing. Naturally, he is heartsick."

"Please convey our sympathies," McCallister said, trying not to sound like the voices he had left behind him at the press conference.

"Of course," said the Russian, nodding for just the right length of time to dispose finally of all feelings of bereavement. Then he continued, trying to build on this mood so well established. "My friend, may I speak frankly?" McCallister's defences were alerted at once. Talk of speaking frankly always had to be listened to with a great deal of caution. Rostov continued: "My government is fearful that an international incident is quite possible here. They request that there be full and complete co-operation between us. Naturally, I assured them that I would be made privy to everything that transpires aboard the space lab."

McCallister shot a look at Mitch Carlino, who looked worried. Rostov caught the exchange, perhaps he saw it coming. He looked at the Director: "There is something I should know?"

McCallister glanced at Dr Leigh, who was trying not to catch his eye. McCallister faced the Russian squarely. "Yes," he said flatly.

"Doctor," interrupted Carlino warningly, trying to help his chief from making this particular disclosure to the Soviet agent.

"Olga Denerenko was murdered," McCallister said simply.

"Jesus!" Carlino could not believe that his chief had actually told the Russian. His eyes were wide with the shock. Dr Leigh, on her part, managed to disguise her emotional reaction. McCallister brought his security director up short.

"Mitch, the Russians have a right to know." He spoke rather sharply, letting Carlino know that this disclosure had not been won from him by Rostov's disarming manner, but represented a thought-out policy on his part. The Russian was trying to assimilate the news.

"Murder?" Rostov searched for eye contact with McCallister. "Doctor, do you know what you are saying?"

"It gives me no pleasure, believe me."

"But *how? Who?*" The seasoned diplomat was at a loss for words. At last he looked at Dr Leigh. She softened toward the Russian and answered his questions as well as she could.

"We were fairly certain the cause of death was asphyxiation . . ."

"Asphyxiation?" the Russian said loudly in the small room, once more the professional. "Quite a change from a brain hemorrhage!"

Margaret Leigh had been expecting this from the moment she had made her false diagnosis known to the Russian. But still, she looked like he had slapped her in the face as she struggled to continue. "We asked Dr Berdoux to examine the body, and with the help of Miss Cooper, he discovered two things. First, faint traces of abrasion around the nose and mouth. Second, three minute white fibres in her respiratory passages."

Rostov looked puzzled as he tried to take the

evidence into his organized mind and label and file each of the items. Margaret continued: "It appears the killer sedated her, then used something to block her breathing — a pillow, glove, towel. We can't tell yet. The material seems to be animal based, maybe wool."

"The killer didn't strangle her," Carlino broke in, attempting to improve on his earlier appearance of obstructing candour. "The marks or bruises would arouse immediate suspicion."

"It was supposed to look like a *natural* death. It almost did," added the Director.

Rostov continued to look shaken. "I see," he said softly. "I shall have to report this to my government." He looked up at McCallister, as though that might prevent further terrible truths. Mitch Carlino broke the silence.

"In a matter of hours, the news will spread throughout the world. Your security's as watertight as a tennis racket."

McCallister wished that Carlino showed more tact on occasions like this. But Rostov shrugged off the remark.

"I regret any embarrassment this may bring to your American commander." He moved toward the door, leaving the implicit threat lying almost palpably in the room. McCallister was quick to pick up the gauntlet.

"I'm afraid we are not the only ones who'll be embarrassed, Alex," he said measuring his words. "At the time of her death, Olga Denerenko was two months pregnant."

Now Rostov showed genuine surprise, shock even. Mitch Carlino drove McCallister's point home. "And once *that* news filters out to the world," the lanky American said, "I'm sure Commissar Denerenko will want to thank you personally for instigating his public humiliation."

Rostov stroked his chin with his large thumb for a moment; when he turned again to face the Americans, he looked almost sunny. "You are right, of course," he said evenly. "This entire matter must be kept confidential. How may I help?"

CHAPTER THIRTEEN

The Chili Chalet was not a place where McCallister thought he would be interrupted. At the same time, the food was more palatable than the fare he was used to at work. Above the counter he could read the full menu. The food was honest here, he thought, even if the log cabin-chalet effect was bogus. McCallister blended into the surroundings, but Carlino's three-piece suit caused a few heads to turn. On top of it, he looked uncomfortable, and squirmed as he watched the Director scoop large spoonfuls from the steaming bowl of chili into his mouth. McCallister's soupstrainer moustache stayed clear of the beans, but it was a near-run contest. Carlino had removed his security clearance tag, but his chief rarely bothered to take his off when he stepped out for half an hour or so. It dangled from his sports coat. Carlino sipped his coffee.

"Andy, tell me something." Carlino finally asked. "What are we doing in this place?" He asked as if McCallister could maybe give the place a history that added up to one madman.

"I'm having supper," McCallister answered between a mouthful. Digging in for another, he said, "You gotta try this chili, Mitch. Best in the West." As he asked Carlino to hand him more crackers, McCallister, with all the knowledge and love of the connoisseur in his voice, began to explain — about the chili, the cumin, the different kinds of chiles, from pasilla and mulato to chipotle and pequin, the tomatoes, the onions . . .

Carlino shook his head as if resigned to not understanding. "We drive six miles so you can have a bowl of chili?"

"No," McCallister said with his mouth full. "So you and I can talk in private while I get to eat something edible."

Carlino drew back. "Anybody who calls that edible is in serious trouble," and waved his arm around the empty room to support his opinion. Finally he laughed, McCallister laughed, and Carlino finished: "So talk."

Putting his spoon down and pushing the bowl to the side, McCallister put his elbows on the table. He took a long breath. "We've got a killer on that ship, and we've got to identify him

before the Delta 216 touches down at Edwards."
He spoke what he'd been thinking and dreaming
for the last forty-eight hours.

"Be simpler to interrogate once they're in
quarantine," Carlino pointed out.

"Mitch, murder is a capital crime, and this
one happened in outer space. You're an ex-
lawyer. Who has jurisdiction to investigate, to
bring charges, to conduct a trial?"

The question didn't expect an answer, but
Carlino was just getting the point. He frowned.
"Maybe nobody. Space law is in its infancy. And
here we've got a space craft that's owned by half
a dozen countries."

"Exactly." McCallister nodded, glad that he had
company in his worries. "So I don't want to de-
pend on legalities. But none of us can manoeuvre
until we know *who* we're talking about."

"Olga's lover?" Carlino wondered.

"Possibly. The question is, did she pick up
with one of those guys during training — during
the flight — or did she know him *before*, from
way back?"

"In other words, we need a history."

"History, yes," McCallister said, "only I don't
mean what we've got on file — I mean her *complete* history. *Everything*."

Carlino thought for a moment. "Rostov could
get it, but I don't trust him. We've got our own
people in Moscow. I'll get it started tonight." He
bit his lip. "Question: How do we find out what's
been going on in the space lab?"

"Through Braddock." Carlino lifted an eyebrow to ask 'why trust anyone?' "Look, I've pretty much told him everything," McCallister explained.

Carlino's eyebrow stayed raised for a moment. "Andy, I know he's a friend — I mean, there's nothin' says he can't be our guy."

McCallister dragged the bowl of chili back in front of him, and lifted his spoon. "I've thought of that," he answered Carlino, and then, as if to end discussion, took another big spoonful of what he described as the stuff with the power to heal.

CHAPTER FOURTEEN

In less than thirty hours, the surviving Conestoga scientists would be on their way back to earth, bringing with them the body of their dead colleague, Olga Denerenko. Shortly after 7:30 Pacific Daylight Time, they would board the Delta 216 shuttle craft attached to the underbelly of the Space Lab. At precisely 7:46, the Delta would separate from the orbiting lab and begin reentry. This would be among the most critical moments of the entire mission. Touchdown at Edwards Air Force Base in Southern California was scheduled for 8:16. The shuttle craft would be piloted by Captain Braddock, or, in the event of his disability, by Colonel Andrei Kalsinov, the remaining Russian cosmonaut.

In the scientific laboratory aboard Conestoga, the work of investigating the murder of Olga Denerenko continued. Pamela Cooper was examining a strand of fibre under a microscope. With great precision, she turned the focusing knob and brought the image into sharpness, making the stained slide reveal the molecular structure of the tiny object on its stage. Pamela closed one of her bright eyes to study the fibre. Behind her a door opened almost noiselessly. But such was the young woman's state that she turned around directly. Leaning in the doorway was the Canadian astronaut, Guy Sterling.

"Sorry, I didn't mean to startle you," he said with a disarming grin.

"I thought I'd locked it," she said simply.

"Really?" said Guy, raising his dark eyebrows. "What's the secret? You're not really trying to identify a Martian plague?" Pamela's lips did not return Sterling's smile. She looked a chill at him across the room and followed it with:

"Guy, please, I really am busy." Guy tried to cut through her impatience with the latest news.

"Well, take a break. Braddock wants everyone on the Command Deck." Guy grinned again, without getting a response, and left the lab. Pamela reluctantly turned off the light illuminating the object stage of the microscope, and replaced the silver plastic cover over the instrument. She looked around the lab abstractedly, then left, setting the lock behind her.

On the Command Deck, the surviving astronauts were assembled. Braddock faced his crew grimly.

"I realize there is still the possibility of error — at least until a physical autopsy can be performed on earth," he said, trying to look at each of the crew in turn. "But at the moment I must operate on the theory that Olga was murdered." With the exception of Pamela and Dr Berdoux, who were already aware of the situation, the others reacted predictably. Steiner was the first.

"Murder? That's insane!"

The Captain tried to calm the former mountain-climber. "I wish it were."

The young Canadian tried to understand the facts: "But how — and *why*, for God's sake?"

"The *how* we know. She was smothered to death. The *why* is a mystery."

Kalsinov, the dead woman's fellow-countryman, looked up at Braddock with cold eyes. "How long have you known this?" Braddock felt Kalsinov adding this, too, to his long list of the Captain's errors in space and on the Martian surface.

"Only a few hours." Braddock looked steadily at the Russian, daring him to ask more. This was his moment to undermine his power, but the Soviet cosmonaut fell silent. Braddock continued. "Eight of us remain aboard this laboratory. Eight and only eight." He looked around from face to face again. "Do I have to spell out the situation?" Steiner looked at Kalsinov. Pamela smiled at the Frenchman, who shrugged. David

Tremayne tried to read the face of the East German, Guy Sterling watched Dominica, whose eyes darted from the Captain to Pamela Cooper. Braddock took a new breath and launched the final stage of his presentation. "I'm going to be in my cabin for the next hour," he announced formally. "If any of you has anything to say — anything at all that may help, please speak up." Braddock thanked the crew for their attention, and moved quickly to the rose-lit passage to his cabin. Before he was quite through the exit, he turned rather theatrically and with a wry smile, made the following suggestion: "Oh, and if the party responsible would like to explain how and why it happened, I'll listen to that too."

Braddock left the remaining seven astronauts in a state of shock. David Tremayne moved automatically to the Guidance Console where he sat down and started checking the readouts. After some hesitation, Guy and Dominica moved down one of the narrow passages toward the Scientific Lab. Pamela watched them go, then crossed to Berdoux, where she sat down near him.

"Are you all right?" she asked.

"I'll be fine, really," the Frenchman said. For a moment, neither of them said anything. Both were thinking over what the Captain had said.

"He shouldn't have told them," Pamela said at length. Berdoux nodded slow agreement.

"Now we will all be thinking — is it he? is it she? Not an ideal situation, considering the teamwork we will need to get down safely." Berdoux paused and looked at Pamela examining her hands, turning them over and over. "All I know," Berdoux continued with a smile, "is that it isn't you. And you know it isn't me. Agreed? Or perhaps neither of us should answer that."

At the Guidance Console David Tremayne had been sitting, staring straight ahead of him, not really examining the print-outs coming through the system. Suddenly, he got to his feet and hurried off the Command Deck and down one of the passageways. His going was noted by Kalsinov and Steiner: Steiner raised an ironic eyebrow; the Russian smiled and moved to the Computer Console to take control of the panel.

Tremayne looked white and sick as he went into his cabin. He carefully closed and locked the door behind him, then headed to the washroom area sink, and threw up. When the dry retching stopped, he was still shaking violently, but fighting to regain control. The outside buzzer sounded; there was someone at his door. His ashen face contorted with pain. He didn't want to talk to anyone. He wanted to be alone. "Who is it?" he called through the thin metal partition. There was no answer. David repeated the question in a louder voice. "Who's there?" Again, silence. Tremayne walked to the door, opened it a crack and peered out. Through the crack he saw the face of Kurt Steiner. Steiner entered David's small cabin without taking his eyes off Tremayne's face. He could see how troubled the young American was. Again, David locked the door behind him. "Are you out of your mind?" he asked in an unsteady voice, sharp with anger. "Someone might have seen you . . ."

"No one saw me . . ." Kurt Steiner said in a flat voice.

"Kurt, we agreed . . ." Steiner could almost smell the fear in Tremayne's speech. He tried to quiet his friend and fellow astronaut.

"I told you, no one saw me." The East German went over to David, who was still trembling slightly. Steiner put his hand gently under David's chin, tipped his face towards his own, and smiled gently. "You're frightened," he said simply. David looked uncertain and didn't say anything. Steiner took David into his arms and held him close. "You are always so fearful," he said not without humour, but with more insight. David broke away from the German's grip and moved away.

"Damn it, Kurt," he said, "I have a right to be." Steiner tried to pour oil, to soothe David's fears.

"No one suspects. I am always careful. Nothing has changed." From these three reassurances, David was able to salvage little.

"Everything's changed. Don't you understand? One of *us* on this ship killed Olga. That means we'll *all* be put under a microscope. It will come out!"

"Not unless we let it," Steiner said with some force. "Her death was unfortunate, but don't ask me to feel pity. She married that old fool in the Kremlin to advance herself, then went around sleeping with any man she could find. Believe me, I know," he said with authority. "Don't tell me she didn't come on with you?" David looked at Steiner and then looked at the clipboard on his bed.

"No," he said with a slight sound of a snarl, "but then I didn't flirt with her the way you did."

"But that's part of my masquerade," Steiner said with a shrug. Then more gently, "David, you must trust me. I have no intention of sharing our relationship with the world. It would hardly do, personally or professionally, to have my private life exposed. It will remain secret by whatever means are necessary." Steiner moved to David again, once more taking him in his arms tenderly and affectionately, stroking his hair gently and holding the young astronaut close to him.

Further along the passageway, Captain Braddock was working in his cabin. It was the largest cabin aboard, since it included some office space as well as the normal, cramped sleeping arrangements. The Captain was working on his logs, when he heard the sound of a knock on his door. He looked up, and wondered whether the criminal was actually out there, ready to confess his deed.

"It's open," he said. Braddock tried to maintain a calm expression as the Russian cosmonaut, Andrei Kalsinov, opened the door and stood just inside the entrance. Kasinov had more of a military bearing than the others, and he could use it to express a wide range of emotions from eager attention to dumb insolence. "Yes?" said the Captain.

"I came," the Russian began slowly, "because I'm sure you regard me as a likely suspect in Olga's death . . ."

"It crossed my mind," the Captain said, putting down his pen, and turning to face his guest. "Particularly since you reacted so violently to the attempts to examine her body."

"Not because I had any idea that murder was involved."

Braddock studied Kalsinov's face, wondering what was written there for the sensitive eye to read. At length, he nodded, "Andrei, Mission Control knows she was pregnant."

Kalsinov's eyes widened as he adjusted to the information. "I wasn't responsible." Braddock was disappointed by the reply.

"No?" he said. "Then who?"

Andrei shifted from his "at ease" stance to a more informal one. It didn't come easily to him, any more than did what he was about to say. "She . . . ," he began slowly, "wouldn't tell me. Look, you and I have had our disagreements, but believe me in this. I didn't get her pregnant and I didn't kill her. It's true that she confided in me. She was terrified."

"Which is why you two were so secretive the past few weeks."

"Yes," the Russian admitted, trying to place his case as simply as he could into these potentially dangerous hands. "She wanted me to arrange an abortion as soon as we returned to Earth." Kalsinov smiled with tight lips. "For you Americans it is a procedure easily obtained. Not so in the Soviet Union, particularly if you are the wife of an important party official."

Braddock nodded agreement. "So if you helped her, you would have been taking a major risk."

The Russian wondered whether he should be saying this. The American was his enemy in every way, and now he was putting himself in the power of one who represented all the qualities he had been trained to scorn and hate. And yet he heard himself make one disclosure after another. He couldn't seem to stop himself. "Olga didn't leave me much choice. She said if I didn't cooperate, she would name me as the father. And, as you perhaps know, Giorgi Denerenko is a violent and jealous man. If he'd learned the truth, he would have had both of us killed."

Again, Braddock found himself nodding. He noticed the action, and stopped it at once. He found that it wasn't difficult to put himself in the Russian's place.

CHAPTER FIFTEEN

In a small, well-kept park on the left bank of
the Moskva River, almost in the shadow of one
of the nineteen great towers of the Kremlin, a
man known to some as Vasilev, was feeding the
pigeons from a brown paper bag. It was early
morning, the park almost empty. The pigeons
flocked in the trodden snow around Vasilev's
feet, fighting for the breadcrumbs like a bunch
of capitalists in a stock exchange. Vasilev shared
his attention with a folded copy of *Pravda*. He
glanced from the story he was reading to the
ever-hungry pigeons. He watched how they often
lost the crumbs to the smaller, swifter sparrows.
He wondered how the sparrows would fit into
his scheme of capitalists grabbing off the bread-

crumbs. His attention was then further subdivided by an approaching male figure. The pigeons took off in a grey flutter as the second man sat on the same park bench, neatly pulling at the creases in the trousers of his Brooks Brothers suit as he did so. This was Roarke. He could be seen at the American Embassy, to which he was as they say, attached. The diplomat also began to feed the birds.

Roarke's embassy work was his cover. His main mission to Moscow was as an operative of the CIA. Similarly, Vasilev was also in the information game, although he was less circumspect than the American. He bought and sold as he could, living the short desperate life of a double agent.

"So, my friend," Vasilev said, without looking up, "what brings us together at this grotesque hour of the morning?"

Roarke looked in the opposite direction from Vasilev's voice. "I presume you weren't followed?"

Vasilev smiled. He was always meeting Americans who reminded him that he represented a vastly older civilization, and Roarke was one of these. "Nor were you, I'm sure. Shall we get to the point?"

"We need to know," the American began, "if there was ever a personal relationship between Andrei Kalsinov and Olga Denerenko."

"You are planning to take political advantage of this tragic situation?" Vasilev sounded hurt.

He could sound sincere when the part he was playing demanded it.

"No. The information may be as helpful to you as it is to us."

"What you are asking is highly dangerous. Colonel Kalsinov is a hero to our people . . ."

The American grinned like a Midwestern farm lad. "And only last year he was considered highly suspect by the KGB."

The Russian shrugged. Some of the pigeons took off in the direction of the Uspenskiy Cathedral within the Kremlin walls. "One premier is forced out, another takes his place. Attitudes change," he said. "Yes, it's true, Colonel Kalsinov was not in favour. But as our most highly qualified cosmonaut, they could hardly keep him from the mission. Even so, they were afraid he might defect. I understand certain precautions were taken to neutralize him had he betrayed his country."

The American let his long hands dangle between his knees, as he tried not looking at Vasilev. "What sort of precautions?"

"The KGB is very resourceful," he said, with another shrug of his rounded shoulders as he hunched over his paper.

"And today, Kalsinov is a hero."

"And Olga Denerenko is a martyr." He paused, thinking of the two of them, one living, one dead, hurtling through space on their way back to Mother Russia by way of the USA. "I'll do what I can," he said, as he scrunched up the empty bag and threw it in the snow for some babushka to pick up. The other continued to watch the pigeons.

Half-way around the world, it was still night at the Mission Control Complex. Judging by the overflowing ashtrays and mutilated styrofoam coffee cups, it had been a busy one. McCallister was sitting at his desk talking on the phone, with half of his attention invested in the VCR which was currently throwing up newsreel footage of Kurt Steiner's sporting exploits on the office TV screen. Mitch Carlino was watching too, and wolfing peanuts from his palm.

"The expedition led by Kurt Steiner reached the summit shortly before one a.m. . . ." the deep voice of an unseen narrator intoned. "These films were taken by fellow climber, Franz Dietrich. It was a record climb for the eight man party . . ." On the screen, Carlino saw Steiner's grizzled face grinning shakily at the camera while holding some kind of flag on the end of his ice axe. McCallister on the phone kept his voice down, speaking in short sentences and nodding at his invisible interlocutor.

"Yes," he said with weight, as though millions lived or died on his choice of words. "No, I don't want that released yet. Braddock's working on it." He paused to listen to the other side, almost failing to see the switch from the Matterhorn to an Olympics skiing site also in Switzerland. The narrator droned on, the voice of a man intoxicated with his own borrowed eloquence.

"Always considered one of the most eligible bachelors on the European ski circuit, Steiner decided to take a stab at the Winter Olympics in Zurich and, to the surprise of everyone, took a gold medal in the men's downhill. Oh, and in case the scarf looks familiar, yes, it's the same one he wore conquering the Matterhorn. Knitted by his mother who died soon afterwards, he considers it a lucky charm . . ." Carlino frowned as the figure on the screen smiled for news photographers with his arms around the shoulders of two laughing girls in pastel ski outfits.

"Arrogant bastard, isn't he?" said Carlino to his chief. McCallister cupped the receiver for a moment and answered:

"Maybe he's got a right to be." Back on the phone, he continued: "No, we still don't have anything concrete on Pamela Cooper. We're waiting on London." He paused for a moment, then grunted and ended the conversation. "I'll get back to you," he said, and hung up.

The VCR machine had been hooked up to the Director's TV set. Together, he and his security director had examined every bit of tape on record about the crew of the Conestoga. McCallister's desk was piled with plastic cassette containers. After watching Steiner send up a blizzard of snow doing a fancy stop in front of the camera, McCallister turned off the TV set. In a continuation of the same effort, he buzzed Dinah in the outer office.

"Yes, sir?"

"Dinah, are you still trying to get through to my wife?"

"Yes, sir," she said in a cigarette-deepened voice. "But the circuits are overloaded." Mc-Callister pondered this for a moment. He was not a man to use privilege on a personal matter. Dinah would never hear the Director ask her to get through on a priority category.

"Keep at it." he said, trying to lift off the gloom of a full night's work from the room. "I suddenly feel like a grandfather."

"Yes, sir," said Dinah, smiling.

At that moment, the door to McCallister's office opened and Margaret Leigh came in carrying some file folders. "Frankly, you don't seem the least bit grandfatherly to me." McCallister looked up with a wide grin on his face.

"So now you're listening in on my private conversations."

"Private?" Dr Leigh repeated, widening her large brown eyes, her face wrinkling into a mass of humorous lines. "We can hear you all the way down the hall." Wearily, she plopped the pile of folders on the Director's desk, not quite seeing the affectionate glance McCallister gave her. "Believe it or not," Margaret said, straightening up from the paper load, "I was not cut out to be a detective."

"Look, you're only one of three people who know the facts — and we want to keep it in the family," Carlino said unnecessarily. "So what did you come up with?"

Margaret looked at Mitch. If she wasn't fond of him, she could have withered him with her gaze. Instead, she smiled like a coquette and brandished a paper from one of the files. "A tidbit from one of your spooks in Rome."

"Rome?" said Carlino, lifting himself off the edge of McCallister's desk with his long arms, and coming towards Margaret. "Something on Dominica Mastrelli?"

"Uh-huh," said Margaret, trying to contain her excitement. "Vis-à-vis she and Olga Denerenko." Carlino's face clouded and he shook his head.

"Sorry, I know for a fact those two never met before this mission was assembled." Margaret looked like she had driven into a brick wall at high speed.

"Do you want to talk or do you want to listen?" she said. She cocked her head and feigned irritation. The Director took charge from the Silex where he had just poured a fresh coffee.

"Don't be a grouch. Just tell us." Coffee in hand, he joined Margaret and Carlino looking at the sheet she had on Dominica Mastrelli.

"Two years ago," Dr Leigh began, "Dominica was having an affair with an Italian professor. A week before he was to have published a breakthrough paper, the identical material appeared in a Russian journal under Olga's by-line." Margaret looked at Carlino and then at McCallister. Neither chose to interrupt. She continued. "Maybe it was coincidence, maybe not. Either way, the professor went off the deep end. Seven months ago he committed suicide. Dominica was with him when he died."

Carlino walked to the other side of the desk and opened a file cover. He studied it for a moment. "Olga had already been named to the team when we got Dominica's application."

"Right," said Margaret crisply. "And Dominica cashed in every marker she had to make sure her government endorsed her application." All three exchanged glances. This was beginning to look like a most promising lead. Not a bad harvest, thought McCallister, for a night's work.

CHAPTER SIXTEEN

Aboard the Space Lab Conestoga, Captain Neal Braddock was conferring with Pamela Cooper. Pamela was explaining about her shortcomings in forensic medicine. "Captain, I can operate a microscope, but I am no expert." Braddock was an amateur at accents, but he could never quite place Pamela's. The up and down inflections suggested something rather horsy and in the Home Counties, but he couldn't put it closer than that, and further, he admitted to himself that he could be dead wrong. Middle class, anyway; he'd bet on that. She continued speaking with the familiar excited lilt to her voice. "I think I have that fibre narrowed down to an animal base — but I can't be more specific."

Braddock nodded in time with the music. But it wasn't her microscope he was interested in at the moment, and his inattention showed in the way he seemed to will her to come to the end of what she was saying. Once she was stopped, the Captain launched himself into the new topic with some energy. "Forget the fibre for a moment," he said, and looked up at the young woman who was leaning over his desk. "I want to talk to you about Olga." Pamela smiled to mask her surprise. "What I need," Braddock continued, "is a woman's insight into her character — *who* she was, *what* she was . . ." Pamela weighed the drift of the inquiry — a shift from the scientific method to womanly intuition.

"We weren't all that close."

"But you were closer than Dominica." Pamela thought about that. She was often amused at the ideas of intimacy among women held by most men. She thought about Olga and Dominica.

"Yes," she admitted. "There was a coolness." Braddock saw that Pamela's eyes were no longer focusing on the here and now. He was about to say something, when she said, almost to herself, "Funny, I remember while we were in training — one night Dominica got a bit drunk and said the strangest thing to me. She said there was someone on the mission who had stolen her life. She said before the trip was over, she'd prove it." Pamela now looked the Captain in the eye. Braddock looked away, smiling.

"I didn't ask you about Dominica."

"But I think Dominica was referring to Olga." Braddock raised his heavy eyebrows. Pamela added, "Merely a guess," and made a pretty shrug.

"Did Olga ever hint at whoever might have gotten her pregnant?"

"No, but . . ."

"But what?"

"I could make a guess."

"Go on." Braddock watched Pamela Cooper composing her words. Giving a report on a fellow crew member was serious, and she wanted to have her feelings and her facts right.

"Olga'd have picked someone safe. Certainly not Andrei." Braddock could feel her running through the faces of her fellow scientists aboard the Space Lab. She didn't hurry in her speech, she was almost teasingly slow. "Ultimately, Andrei'd have been more loyal to Mother Russia than to her. Kurt Steiner? A braggart and a talker. Much too risky. And you can eliminate Dr Berdoux as well."

"Because of his age?" Braddock soon wished he'd chosen his words more carefully. Pamela's eyes flashed with anger.

"Because he is not the sort of man to get involved with someone like *her*. He has been happily — and faithfully — married to his wife for twenty-nine years." Braddock felt that he got off lightly under the circumstances. Berdoux had an ally aboard the Space Lab whose loyalty amounted to more than that of one scientist to another. The Captain didn't chase it. He went on quickly:

"All right. That leaves David Tremayne and Guy Sterling . . ."

"And, of course, *you*, Captain."

"I'm flattered," said Braddock smiling. Pamela couldn't decide whether or not the Captain blushed a little around the gills. She went on:

"For several reasons, I'd say it was Guy. Married or not, he likes the ladies. For the first three weeks of training, he tried to move in on me. He even went so far as to tell me he'd had a vasectomy."

"You're kidding." Braddock hadn't heard that line used since his freshman days, and even then, it got the horselaugh except from the most backward and unsophisticated.

"Not at all."

"I wonder," the Captain said thoughtfully, "if he used that line on Olga . . ."

"It's possible," said Pamela, thinking over what she knew about both Olga and the Canadian. Braddock got up from his seat against the wall of his cabin. Pamela was slightly surprised at this note of civility in the Captain.

"Thank you, Pamela," he said. "You've been very helpful." Pamela straightened up, and made for the door in a businesslike way. But she stopped when she had her hand on the handle, and turned to face the Captain.

"Sir, this TV press conference later on," she asked. "Must we?" She looked for signs of sym-

pathy in the Captain's expression. "I mean, it
seems so grotesque — pretending to the world
that everything's all right when we know bloody
well one of us is a killer." Braddock tried hard
to smile. He knew how close he came to sharing
Cooper's feelings, but he — not she — had the
command of Conestoga, and with command
came all sorts of unpleasant duties.

"It's necessary," he said gently. "We're under
orders to pacify the media."

Pamela nodded sadly and left the cabin. Braddock looked after her for a moment, then
frowned down on the piece of paper before him
on the desk. It contained brief notes and doodles.
Among the things to be read there was the name,
Guy Sterling. As he looked at the name again,
Braddock took up his pencil again and drew a
circle around it.

CHAPTER SEVENTEEN

Inside the International Space Exploration Administration's Mission Control Complex, the lights were burning late into the night. Along the corridor of the Director, the lights had not been turned off for the last forty-eight hours at least. In his private office, McCallister was sitting at his desk, reading and trying to eat a sandwich Dinah had brought to him some hours ago. When he looked up over the rye-bread crusts, he saw the wife of David Tremayne, one of his astronauts, standing in the doorway. McCallister was suddenly filled with the horrible thought that he had been neglecting the whole human and compassionate side of this fantastic crime. What about the people who care about the crew up there? he thought. To them they aren't suspects, but husbands and loved ones.

"Dr McCallister?" Irene Tremayne said, almost in a whisper. The Director looked at her haggard face, and struggled awkwardly to his feet.

"Oh, Mrs Tremayne . . ."

"Please don't stand," she said self-deprecatingly. "Excuse me — really, I don't want to bother you — but — may I sit down?"

"Sure." Irene Tremayne moved to the indicated chair to one side of his desk and McCallister moved his own chair so that there was as little of the formal atmosphere between them as possible. On a thought, McCallister looked at his wrist watch. "Aren't you supposed to be getting ready for the TV cameras?"

"I have a few minutes," she said, trying to smile. McCallister suddenly felt deserted by his usually easy manners. He heard himself offer Mrs Tremayne some coffee and cake, but to his inner ear it sounded hollow and self-important, all at the same time. Irene Tremayne shook her head. He could see that there was something on her mind that she needed to say. He tried to make himself look quiet and concentrated. After a moment, she began to speak.

"I . . . uh, I spent a couple of hours this afternoon being interviewed by a man named Carlino," she said. McCallister nodded to her encouragingly. "His questions were personal, Doctor — having to do with my marriage, my sex life — I felt humiliated."

McCallister looked at her sitting in front of him. He could see the truth of her words written all over her. And, of course, he knew what Carlino was doing. He didn't like it, but he knew it had to be done. All he could say was, "I'm sorry."

"He also hinted," Irene continued, "that David may have had something to do with Olga Denerenko's death. Some kind of love affair."

McCallister breathed easier. He was able to say with complete honesty, "Afraid I don't know anything about that."

Irene searched the face of the Director. Could she trust him, she wondered. Was this the kind of face she could believe in? She hesitated, looking troubled, as if wrestling with her conscience. Then she reached into her purse and took out an envelope. It was the envelope that she had kept in her suitcase, the one she had hidden the night Guy Sterling's wife came by to talk to her in the hotel. She turned the letter over in her hand as she spoke, not looking at the Director. "David sent me this letter," she began in a low groping voice, "only hours before the spacecraft lifted off for Mars." She held the letter out to McCallister, looking up at him for the first time since she mentioned the letter. McCallister took the paper from her and adjusted his glasses. Removing the folded paper from the envelope, he studied the contents.

"You will see, Dr McCallister," she said, "the idea that David could be involved with that Russian woman in a sexual way — it seems a little absurd. For the past year, David and I did not make love for the simple reason that he was not interested. I blamed myself," she said, stretching the words, and then added in a lower voice, "and then I received this. I suppose it was partly his way of making me feel less guilty . . ." Irene Tremayne looked very little in McCallister's office, rather woebegone and wistful. She added: "Near the end, he says he wants a divorce. Something quiet and discreet without embarrassment to either of us." McCallister finished the letter in silence. He looked shocked and surprised, but looked at Irene Tremayne with a breadth of human sympathy that had nothing to do with his large responsibilities.

"I'm sorry, Mrs Tremayne," he said, pressing her hand with feeling. He thought of fragments of other things to say, but he could put them in no order before Irene, herself, shrugged and went on.

"Well, these things happen, don't they, Doctor?" she said with a brave little smile. "Usually, however, to someone else."

McCallister went back over the letter. "He doesn't identify his new . . . friend — except for this one reference . . ." He began to hunt for the passage. "'He is bright — clever — an extrovert who makes a show of being a ladies' man though he has nothing but contempt for them.'" McCallister stroked his chin, as his mind played over the possibilities.

"It could be someone aboard the mission," Irene suggested. She hadn't really thought much about trying to identify her husband's lover. Her interest had been in clearing him as a possible suspect in Olga Denerenko's death. "The problem really began when he was in training."

Irene Tremayne rose from the chair, obviously fighting back the tears. McCallister got up as well and came around to take the woman's arm. "Doctor, I've shown you that," indicating the letter which McCallister was returning to its envelope, "for only one reason. I love my husband and I intend to fight for him. I hope I've done the right thing."

McCallister put the envelope back into Irene's hand. "I promise you, Mrs Tremayne," he said in a voice that she could believe, "no one will know the contents of this letter unless it's absolutely necessary."

"Thank you." She blinked, as though trying to get something off her eyelashes. "Isn't it funny?" she continued, putting on her gloves, "in a few minutes, David and I will be performing before tens of millions of people, pretending to be the All-American couple. I'm not sure I can pull it off." She turned, and hurried away. McCallister watched her go, then returned to his desk and his remaining snack. He looked at the food, suddenly no longer hungry. He shoved the tray away.

CHAPTER EIGHTEEN

The Communications Center of Mission Control Complex was looking, in one part, like any TV studio set up for an afternoon talk show. Sitting around a small coffee table, directly in front of the Center's TV screen, were the patient wives of the daring crew, Irene Tremayne and Eleanor Sterling. Between them, looking lively, relaxed and professional, was Jeffrey Kilbride. With a smile at Irene, he had just turned to David Tremayne, his face filling the large screen, to ask the weary venturer about his thoughts of home and family. The studio camera closed in on Tremayne's image.

"Well," Tremayne answered, a look of strain perceptible behind his camera-ready cheer, "to tell you the truth, I've been thinking about hot turkey, cranberry sauce . . ."

The second camera swung round abruptly to focus in on Irene, who was now all hearty mother and wife. "Well, I think I could arrange that. 'Course Mom'll want to make the stuffing."

McCallister had been standing at the back of the room, watching intently, an image of cranberry sauce, a naked dead body and blood gravy taking hold in his mind, the image all mixed up with thoughts about the great American family as a TV invention.

"Well, that's nice," Tremayne was answering his wife. His next statement seemed a bid to end the interview. "Say 'hi' for me when you talk to her."

Rostov, working at a desk in another corner of the Communications Center, was perhaps uninterested in American gastronomical fantasies and familial affections. As Kilbride asked: "David, excuse me, but do you think you've lost any weight?" Rostov glanced up at the screen for a moment, but his attention was back to his work before David answered.

"Oh," he said, "I'd say for sure. There's not much to snack on even if you wanted to."

Kilbride laughed easily, and glanced to the two women, who as if on cue smiled politely. He then prodded David for more of his plans on returning home. David joined in, playing along like the good sport he was, but again, there was the evidence of strain. "I thought maybe we could take off for a couple of weeks — go to Vermont —" the second camera shifted to Irene for reaction shots as David went on: "That old cabin by the lake, you remember, with the leaky boat —"

"And the leaky roof?" Irene interrupted, laughing.

"Right," David said, stretching out the word as he laughed and groaned.

Suddenly, behind the laughing face of Tremayne, a figure lurched into view, gasping. David jumped up, as the figure, grabbing at a console to stop his fall, cried out. At the Center, McCallister had stiffened for a moment, then moved toward the screen, while it was Eleanor Sterling, rising slowly, who was the first to recognize the heaving figure. Braddock had by now come into view, running, and both he and Eleanor spoke in the same moment: "Guy?" Guy Sterling fell forward and rolled on his back, as both David and Braddock knelt over him. "Doctor!" Braddock screamed, while back at Mission Control, Eleanor, unmoving, screamed "Guy!" again.

Kilbride, seeing in the horror nothing but a better story than the one he'd just been telling, asked, his voice filled with professional urgency: "Captain Braddock, can you hear me? Can you tell us what's happening?" But McCallister, yelling at one of the technicians and looking knives at Kilbride, ordered, "Cut the network feed! Now, damn it, cut it!"

The rest was all confusion. Aboard the space craft a hand moved to cover the lens of the camera momentarily, cutting out some of the picture. A technician reached forward to throw a switch and Rostov raced out of the room, while Eleanor Sterling watched the large TV set, heard the scream of panic, as Irene held her. Eleanor saw a woman rushing to Guy's side, to his inert body. She saw the woman start to pound on his chest, giving orders to another man simultaneously. "Tell Dr Berdoux!" the woman said sharply. Her voice rose, "I need ten cc's of adrenalin – now!"

Meanwhile, in the Center itself, McCallister was shouting, waving his arm around the room: "I want this room cleared now! All civilians and press – please leave immediately." Carlino, who'd come rushing in as Rostov left, spoke into the intercom: "Get security in here now!" and was then echoing McCallister: "Clear the room!" McCallister had by now reached his main target, and with his hand placed firmly on Kilbride's shoulder, instructed him in no uncertain terms, "I'm sorry, you've got to leave –"

"Damn it, McCallister," Kilbride almost whined with disappointment, "what the hell's going on up there?"

"Mitch," – McCallister was having none of it – "get this guy out of here!" Carlino moved quickly to escort the unwilling Kilbride from the room, while the four armed security guards who had just entered were herding the "non-essen-

tials" in the direction of the door. McCallister
now took Eleanor gently by the arm. "Mrs Sterling," he said softly, "please go to a holding
room. You shouldn't have to watch this. We'll
keep you informed."

Eleanor was looking around as if dazed. "My
husband," she said to McCallister, as if he could
explain, "Guy —"

McCallister's voice stayed steady: "They're
doing everything they can," he said, and with
the help of Irene Tremayne, lead Eleanor to the
exit.

Leaving Eleanor with Irene and two guards,
McCallister looked back at the large TV screen.
He saw Berdoux come into the room and kneel
down by Guy's side. The doctor examined Sterling's eyes before unsheathing a large hypo of
adrenalin. He plunged it hard into the man's
heart.

In seconds Berdoux had withdrawn the
needle, leaned into Guy's face, rechecked his
pupils. Straightening, he looked up at Braddock
who asked, "What is it?" Berdoux sighed, hesitated, "I . . . I can't be sure." He closed his eyes
for a moment, then opened them as he spoke
again: "I think perhaps poison, Captain." Braddock, as if unable to understand, bent over to see
where, on Guy's bare arm, something — a
needle — had left a puncture hole, to see the
droplet of blood that had dried around it.

Suddenly, Braddock swung up and around to
face the camera. "Andy," he snapped, "cut this

transmission." In the Communications Center McCallister turned sharply to a technician, shouting, "Do it! Now!"

The technician flipped a switch. The picture was gone.

In the Conestoga, Braddock was racing from the Command Deck, through the corridors, followed closely by Kalsinov and Pamela. He suddenly swerved, darting into the open doorway of Guy Sterling's cabin. He was on his knees, his hands searching the floor. At the foot of the bed, hidden just behind one leg, there it was. Braddock, still on his knees, straightened up, holding now a hypodermic needle and a small medical vial. Pamela and Kalsinov bent over. The three stared at the vial as Braddock turned it slowly between his fingers. Its label read "INSULIN".

CHAPTER NINETEEN

Braddock's worried face appeared on the TV screen in the Director's office. It was looking McCallister in the eye, and a reverse angle shot in a film would have confirmed this. But the face on the screen wasn't in a movie, and the appearance of eye-to-eye contact was an illusion. Braddock could see McCallister all right, but when he glanced at his monitor aboard Conestoga, he appeared to be looking away from the camera on the Director's screen. To Carlino, who stood near his chief, both Braddock and McCallister were showing the strain of the last three days. Of the two, he'd say that Braddock looked the least frazzled, but he had twenty years on his chief and he had already absorbed the shock of five months in space and on the Martian surface.

Braddock was alone in his cabin, and both he and McCallister were using one of the scrambler circuits. Each sat in front of a high-mounted, fixed camera and was bombarded with floodlights. The resulting images were rather flat and shadowless; the faces looked washed out and featureless. "Cyanide," Captain Braddock said.

McCallister winced at the thought and asked, "You're sure?"

"Berdoux's convinced, and Pam Cooper backs him up," he said. "It was in the insulin. As soon as Guy injected himself, he never had a chance."

Mitch Carlino leaned into the frame beside his chief, and at once the familiar face was in Braddock's cabin on his monitor. "Who could have gotten to his insulin supply, Captain?"

Braddock considered the question for a moment, then made half a shrug. "Any of us." He looked at McCallister on the screen. "Look, Andy, my people know what's going on and believe me, they are damned scared." He paused to make his pitch, and then he made it: "Andy, I want to come down *now*."

"We're not prepared for that . . ."

"Well *get* prepared," insisted the Captain of the Space Lab. "We have a lunatic loose up here. Kalsinov's running a pre-check on the Delta 216 right now."

Braddock watched McCallister take a measured breath. "You can't risk a premature separation. You may not have enough fuel."

"Whatever the risk, it's less than staying up here."

McCallister weighed the new situation and Braddock's assessment of it. In the end, he nodded agreement. "All right. I'll do what I can," he said, trying to get across an impression of the solid back-up Mission Control would put behind this unscheduled re-entry.

"And soon," added Braddock. "Out." Braddock pushed a button on the control panel and the screen went black. As he leaned back in his chair, he looked troubled. The dilemma facing him was clear: the risk of an unwise premature re-entry, putting all of the remaining lives in hazard, or waiting out the normal operation plan and hoping against hope that the killer would not strike again. No wonder his face looked troubled.

The early morning sun streamed through the curtains of the hotel's vice-presidential suite illuminating trays with plates of discarded soft-boiled egg shells, toast crusts, and packages of plastic-wrapped jam and marmalade. The men sitting in the room had been up before the sun. The Vice-President, who was not yet dressed or shaved, sat on the edge of a settee. Mitch Carlino and Andrew McCallister were dressed, but it was clear that they were wearing yesterday's clothes. In deference to the Veep's high office, McCallister had put on a necktie. It was pink. The Veep was saying, "Then there's no doubt the man was poisoned?" He looked from Carlino to McCallister.

"None, sir," he said. "Our computers verified the contents. One vial had been tampered with. It contained a lethal amount of CCA — a cyanide compound often used by intelligence agents in the event of capture."

"Like a suicide capsule?"

"Yes, sir." Mitch Carlino added an explanation.

"The Russians issue those things to their military people as a matter of course." The Veep nodded a thank you in the direction of Mitch, then turned back to the Director.

"Andy, we've got to bring them down."

"That's Captain Braddock's intention, sir," said McCallister, whose words brought a lessening of tension around the mouth of the Vice-President.

"Good," he said. "And, Andy, impress upon him the need for caution. He is to maintain the tightest security possible. I want the rest of those people back alive."

Some hours later, McCallister was eating a sandwich. He couldn't put a name to the meal. Whether it was lunch or dinner had no meaning when hours become as scrambled as his had. Nor could he taste what he was eating. He knew that he had to keep the engine working, and so he ate, but he took no pleasure in it as he watched the six o'clock news on the TV screen. An unseen voice heard over a picture of the news room set was speaking. "UCS News presents the Six

O'clock Report. Now, live from the Mission Control Complex, here is correspondent Jeffrey Kilbride."

The picture switched to the familiar landmarks, the facade of the Complex and Kilbride. The reporter stood with a hand microphone and looked into the camera. "A veil of secrecy now shrouds Mission Control . . ." he began. McCallister chewed and reflected on his decision to exclude the press. He'd been right, he thought. Kilbride continued. "For nearly six hours there has been no news of Guy Sterling, the Canadian meteorologist who collapsed on the Space Lab's command deck — a collapse witnessed briefly by hundreds of millions of shocked viewers. Is Sterling alive or dead? No one will say." McCallister's jaw hardened as Kilbride continued to lay it on with a trowel. "And if he is ill or disabled, is there any connection to the death of Olga Denerenko two days ago? Suddenly, what seemed like a fantasy from a science fiction movie has become a stark and ugly possibility — that somehow the crew of the Conestoga is being attacked by a deadly virus from outer space." McCallister took a swallow from his umpteenth cup of coffee and turned off Kilbride and his report to the nation.

A few minutes later, on the screen of a computer in the Command Center, the word CHLOROCYANTICALUMITE flashed into view. Her eyes tight on the screen, Dr Margaret Leigh watched the chemical symbols for the substance write themselves beneath the name of the poison. Margaret picked up the telephone and dialled McCallister's private line. "Dr McCallister," she said when she was sure that it was indeed the Director that she had at the other end, "I've got that information on the cyanide. The file confirms it is highly toxic and causes almost instant death. Gel capsules — the type used by the Russians — come in various sizes depending on the body weight of the subject. The most typical dosage for their foreign agents is five cc's, which will kill a male of average size and weight within ten seconds."

At his end of the line, McCallister acknowledged the information, and immediately began getting in touch with Braddock again on the scrambler. When the hook-up was completed, McCallister took his place in the floodlit chair with the red light of the TV camera shining down at him. In his lap, the Director carried a pile of file folders. Even to Braddock, many thousands of miles out in space, the signs of utter exhaustion were clear. McCallister was speaking. "It's been checked and double-checked. The computer confirms the poison is a special favourite of the Russians. Both Olga and Kalsinov might have been issued dosages before the mission to be used in case — in case of what? Attack by Martians? Jesus, I'm not even thinking straight any more."

Braddock smiled. "You're thinking better than you look."

McCallister grinned back at Braddock. "Must have been that eight minute nap I took." The Director moved his hand over the haggard face trying to pull away, it seemed, all of the debilitating effects of age and sleeplessness. It didn't work. "Neal," he continued, "have you figured out who David Tremayne's boyfriend is yet?"

Braddock looked thoughtful, then shrugged, "It's got to be Kurt Steiner, though to tell you the truth, I never suspected he was homosexual. I don't think any of us did." He paused, watching McCallister look into a file folder at his end. "Anyway," Captain Braddock concluded, "I'm not sure it has any bearing."

"Maybe it doesn't," the Director retorted. "I'm grasping." To Braddock, the haggard-looking man on the screen in front of him suddenly looked stronger than he had. Braddock thought for a moment about the guts the old man had. Meanwhile, McCallister was back at him: "Look, Neal, the only thing that counts right now is the safety of the crew." The Director added as a wry afterthought: "Even if it means letting the killer get off."

"That's hardly a possibility," said Braddock.

"Don't be so sure. Suppose we find him? Who's going to prosecute? Who has jurisdiction? The minute you touch down, the killer may be home free."

"That's obscene," said Braddock coldly. He had not thought of the outer-space loophole in the law.

"Maybe," said McCallister. "But there's nothing either one of us can do about it. Anyway — good luck. Out."

A moment before McCallister's face was due to disappear from the screen, Neal Braddock asked the old man, "Andy? You haven't mentioned Jill's baby. No news yet?"

The Director's face broke into a smile that came up from fifty fathoms. "You wanna know something? Right now, I'm not even sure she's pregnant. Out." McCallister broke off the communication at that point. He watched the familiar face of the Captain break up into a thousand lines. In his cabin aboard Conestoga, Captain Braddock flipped off his switch, and hesitated for a thoughtful minute.

CHAPTER TWENTY

A black unmarked car, blacker than the Moscow night, pulled up to the high gate of Russian Commissar Giorgi Denerenko's heavily guarded house. While the four topcoated figures who stood in the shadows watched, the armed security guard at the front gate bent to the car window. A few questions were asked and answered, the identification papers of the men inside the car checked quickly. With a nod from the guard, the car moved through the gate, down the drive, and to a stop at the front door. A man, attaché case in his hand, hurried out of the car and to the door.

Inside, a few minutes later, Denerenko was staring in disbelief at the young deputy sent with the news. Although the living room offered every comfort with its soft chairs, sofas, divans, neither man had sat through the interview. "You're absolutely sure of this?" Denerenko said at last, his heavy jowls quivering, giving him an oddly frail look. He had wanted to force the young, exact and efficient official to say it wasn't so. He knew before he started that he would fail.

"Yes, sir," the deputy answered. He had an annoying habit, Denerenko now thought, of speaking as though simply reading his lines from a script. "The cause of her death has been confirmed without question."

Denerenko paused, not for the first time in this interview. He finally said, or asked, or begged — he didn't know which — "Murder?"

"Yes, sir," the deputy said mechanically.

Denerenko started to turn toward the door of the living room, stopped, turned back and moved to the window. For several minutes he stood looking out, perhaps wondering at the gates and locks and armoury that protected him — that could not protect him from this. When he turned back to face the messenger, it was with a grim but accepting look on his face, his lips thin and tight, his eyes narrowed. "There is more," he said, "isn't there?" He expected the sudden discomfort the deputy showed, simply snorting as the man shifted from one foot to the other, saying, "We are not sure, sir —"

"Tell me!" Denerenko demanded. He would know it, he would accept it — all Denerenko now asked was that he be told *what* he must know, *what* he must accept. He waited, his expression repeating his demand.

"There is a report . . . there is speculation . . ." The deputy took one large breath. It was as if, Denerenko thought, he had lost his place for a moment in the script. "Sir," the man said at last, running on now, "the Americans believe your wife was two months pregnant at the time of her death. Naturally, the idea is preposterous — certainly the autopsy will disprove such an insulting suggestion."

Denerenko suddenly moved toward the deputy, his large body threatening. "Now, even in death, she has dishonoured me," he said softly, quickly, as if his own anger was the last surprise. And then he turned away, just as suddenly. No fact, no feeling would defeat him. From the cigar box on his desk top he took a cigar, an expensive Havana, the only kind he smoked. He rolled it round in his fingers, watching it, then returned it to the box. "The Delta 216 is scheduled to land in less than ten hours," he said, and the deputy answered, "Yes, sir." Denerenko spoke with his old ease. "Is it possible to contact Colonel Kalsinov? Without the knowledge of the others?"

The deputy, now given a role as helper rather than messenger of bad tidings, relaxed a little. He looked more directly at the Commissar. "Perhaps, sir. We would have to go through Alexander Rostov."

"Do it," Denerenko said abruptly. "Have Rostov make it clear to Colonel Kalsinov that I wish the Delta 216 diverted to a landing site within the Soviet Union."

The deputy looked down again, shifted uneasily. He hesitated before saying quietly, "Sir, that is impossible."

"*Make* it possible!" Denerenko ordered. This was anger controlled by a purpose. "Do whatever you have to, but *under no circumstances* will my wife's body be defiled by the Americans."

The deputy's face was now a mask. "Yes, sir."

CHAPTER TWENTY-ONE

McCallister stood just behind the main technician, waiting, watching; strangely, he remembered his mother's rather sad comment on her son's disappointments, both small and large. "If only wishing could make it so," she'd say, and he now thought, yes, if only. Final preparations were underway for separation of the Delta 216 and the return to Earth. McCallister looked around for the hundredth time to see that all the technicians were alert at their computers. He stared for several minutes at the large TV screen. There were the images of Pamela Cooper and David Tremayne, manning the computer on the Conestoga Command Deck, checking and cross-checking the re-entry procedures with the ground crew here at Mission Control.

McCallister wasn't reassured by Tremayne's calm, confident tone. "Control," the young man's voice came across clearly, "I'd like a confirmation on horizontal attitude." McCallister knew the reading by heart. "Reading five," Tremayne intoned, "eight-nine-six-point-three-four."

Another minute passed and the technician sitting in front of McCallister responded. "That's a roger, David." The technician looked across to the upper left-hand panel, McCallister's eyes following his. "Will you activate your Z-valve readouts. We may have a problem with compression in one of the forward jets." Again, McCallister's eyes trailed the technician's as the readouts came across the central screen.

A second check and the technican was swivelling round to face the Director, smiling, saying, "With luck . . . and enough fuel . . . they'll be home for breakfast." But Andy McCallister wasn't smelling bacon and eggs, but diesel; he wasn't believing in luck but in fuel measures and the things that go wrong at the last minute. That was his anxious mother again, it was, "you can never be too careful" and, "I wouldn't count on it, Andrew." McCallister sighed. "Let's hope," was all he said.

In another sector of Mission Control, down several winding corridors from the Communications Center and behind a door marked SECURITY, Mitch Carlino was demanding of the elderly army captain why, in hell, he'd been called away from re-entry preparations. "All

right, Captain," he said snappishly, "what's
so urgent?"

"Courier, sir," the stolid captain answered;
he'd stood up when Carlino'd entered but beyond that it appeared he wasn't going to get excited — not if the courier in his office was the
Angel Gabriel himself and Carlino late for the
trumpet call. With a nod, the Captain intro-
duced Carlino to the courier and the courier to
Carlino, then accepting his job as done, stepped
back while the two men exchanged glances. The
courier's was nothing if not self-important, Carlino's simply puzzled.

"What's this all about?" Carlino demanded,
as the courier rather laboriously unlocked the
chain that attached a brown briefcase to his
wrist, and handed the briefcase to ISEA's Director of Security. "Special file, sir," the courier said in a voice lowered several octaves for
this important occasion. "Code name Hammer,
through Blue Sector."

Carlino seemed to take a minute to process the
information, then, with a shake of his head,
went to work. Setting the briefcase on the desk,
he took out a small blue notebook from his
pocket. He flipped through its well-thumbed
pages until coming to a halt. He read what was
on the page once with his eyes, then again, but
with his lips moving silently. Done, he'd set five
numbers on the briefcase's combination lock,
the lock opened with a clicking sound. Only one
slight blue file lay within, a file that would,

Carlino now presumed, explain exactly what in the hell was so urgent.

McCallister watched her for a moment, still sitting behind her desk, a pen between two fingers — but her head was in her hands as she dozed, dreaming of beds and comforters, McCallister supposed. It was when he tried, impossibly, to tip-toe by that Dinah woke, coming to with a start and a blush. McCallister stopped as if he himself had been caught out in some mischief. Smiling at his devoted secretary, his voice low, he said: "Dinah, I love you dearly but go home and get some sleep." Dinah's rather gruff answer, the slight tilting of her chin, were meant to remind both her boss and herself that a night's sleep missed was just part of the job. "I'll sleep tomorrow," she said simply, and then, in an undertone, "You've got company."

Mitch Carlino, the company that awaited McCallister in his office, was anything but dozy. But as McCallister moved quickly to the scrambler TV, saying, "Eight more hours, Mitch. Count 'em. *Eight*," he wasn't noticing his friend's agitation, how he sat forward on the edge of his chair as though it were up to him to count out every second of those eight hours himself.

"Andy," Carlino interrupted the Director, "before you activate that thing, there's something you'd better know." McCallister stopped in his tracks; Carlino waited for his own concern to be felt. Finally, handing McCallister a folded

sheaf of papers, he said, "Read this," for the first
time sinking back in his chair while McCallister
readjusted his glasses. One hand still tracking
the desk top, McCallister squinted at the papers.
"Looks like something you tore out of the telephone book," he said — at last, his hand found
what he needed.

"It's Olga Denerenko's secret Soviet File,"
Carlino answered, and McCallister, his glasses
now firmly planted on his nose, looked again at
the papers. Surprise slowly possessed his, until
then, myopic expression. He sat down with a
thud and a groan. "How'd you get it?" he asked.

"Never mind," Carlino said shortly, coming to
the point that needed no further sharpening.
"Fifteen years ago, Olga Denerenko was nineteen, living in London. Her father was a minor
bureaucrat assigned to the Soviet's London Embassy." This was, McCallister thought, Carlino
the quick study, the memory machine invented,
patented and produced in the thousands by your
friendly CIA. Carlino had indeed done his
homework: "About a dozen students from Ox-
ford were invited to an Embassy reception. One
of those students was an American Rhodes
scholar named Neal Braddock. She and Braddock began seeing each other." Carlino paused
as McCallister closed his eyes for a minute, seeing his friend Braddock seeing Olga Denerenko. Carlino picked up the story. "Their meetings
were supposed to be secret, but the KGB was on
her ass from day one." More likely from day
zero, McCallister thought. "Apparently," Car-

lino said, "it had nothing to do with politics, just sex."

"Her father was reassigned to Moscow and Olga returned with him." Carlino, the CIA, the KGB, McCallister thought, feeling his own exhaustion, they were all of them tireless. "Braddock went back to the U.S. and that was the end of it. As far as the Russians are aware, they didn't see each other again until the start of the Conestoga Space Mission."

McCallister, unable to hear more, suddenly lunged forward in his chair. "Great, Mitch," he said angrily. "Your boys do a backgrounder on both her *and* Captain Braddock and you come up with zilch."

"Or so you hope, Andy," was what Carlino said to himself. To McCallister, he spoke to placate. "Okay," he said easily, "we missed it. I'm sorry." Carlino saw his friend's body become limp, a victim of anger and confusion that had no place to go. "Look," Carlino went on, "she was a schoolgirl, her name was different, he wasn't yet attached to the military." Carlino tried a half-smile. "It slipped through the cracks."

Now, McCallister thought, coming out as the worms in the woodwork. "Yeah," he said in a voice leaden with anger, the kind that fears it's been tricked, diverted off course, "and not once did Braddock tell us he'd known her before." McCallister waited. He stared for a minute at Carlino. He stared at the blank TV screen. Finally, he asked, "Why not?"

In another minute — of silence between Mc-

Callister and Carlino — a picture came up on the screen, a picture showing Braddock's cabin, empty, that seemed to prod McCallister into action. "I'll beep him," he said as he reached toward a red button, and as his finger came down hard on CALL PAGE, he thought how it was, as usual, a case of "Know thy enemy."

CHAPTER TWENTY-TWO

The radio pager attached to Captain Braddock's belt began to flash red and beep quietly. Without looking down, his hand turned off the signal. McCallister can wait a minute, he thought.

With him on the Command Deck of the Space Lab were six of the remaining seven astronauts. Only one of the crew was missing. Braddock looked annoyed. "Where's Steiner?" he asked generally. "Has anyone seen him?"

"Not for a while," offered David Tremayne.

"Dominica," Braddock ordered, letting a little of his annoyance with Steiner adhere to this request, "check his cabin. Get him here on the double."

"Yes, sir." Dominica left the Command Deck almost noiselessly, but on the double. Her way led her down a passageway and around a corner. She stopped outside Steiner's door and knocked. She waited to hear noises within, but there were none. No sleepy voice pulled out of a dream, asking who wanted him. There was no answer at all. Dominica knocked again, louder this time, feeling the pain in her knuckles. Still no answer. "Kurt?" she called, and banged on the door harder still. Again, there was no response. Her hand moved in the direction of the door buttons. She tried them and the door slid open. Dominica looked inside the cabin. "Kurt?" she called again. The cabin was small enough so that it would be difficult to miss someone if that someone were there. Dominica was in the act of turning and reaching for the door again when she saw it. Her eyes widened with the horror of what was now etching itself into her retinas. The terror in the scream that escaped her, nearly rattled the rivets of the Space Lab.

Back on the Command Deck, the scream pierced the silence. In a flash, the Captain was on his feet and flying down the passageway with the others at his heels. Half way there, he ran into a bewildered Dominica coming out of Steiner's cabin. She was still screaming hysterically, when Pamela Cooper grabbed the woman by her arms and shook her sharply. Braddock demanded: "What is it? What happened?"

Dominica was only able to say through her tears, "Oh, God! Oh, God!" Braddock pushed

past her in the corridor with Kalsinov right behind him. Meanwhile, Pamela was trying to get
sense out of the frightened girl.

"Dominica — what is it? What happened?"

"Steiner . . ." was all she could blurt out.

"What about him?" Pamela urged, but already sensing the terrible answer.

Braddock and Kalsinov entered the shambles
that Steiner's cabin had become. Papers and
equipment were all over the floor and cot. A terrible struggle had taken place here, judging by
the broken picture frames and the bent side of
his desk. On the floor they saw the reason for
Dominica's scream and the explanation of Steiner's failure to muster to the Command Deck with
the others. Kurt Steiner lay on his back, with his
eyes staring at the ceiling, his white wool scarf
tied sufficiently tightly around his neck to make
the cause of Steiner's deathly silence clear. His
hands, now frozen still, were clutching at the
strangling loop of scarf around his neck. Braddock and Kalsinov moved to Steiner's side. The
Captain examined the scarf, then looked up at
Kalsinov. "His lucky scarf," he said. With his
fingers, he tried to loosen the constriction. There
was no question about whether or not the East
German was dead. The engorged face above the
ligature was testimony enough.

"I thought he was going to plant it on Mars
like a flag," the Russian said. Braddock looked
over the body at him. "Apparently, he changed
his mind."

Dr Berdoux pushing into the cabin, stood for

a moment in the doorway to take in the scene, then joined the others by the body. "Let me see," he said. Kalsinov curled his lip at the Frenchman.

"See with what, Doctor?" he rasped, letting it carry away some of the Russian's feeling of anger and frustration. "You're half blind. We all know it." Berdoux looked up sharply. He was embarrassed and angry at the Russian for bringing his private affliction into the public arena. Before he could answer, Kalsinov grabbed the Frenchman's hands and pressed them roughly against the cheeks of the dead man. "He's already starting to turn *cold*. He's *dead*, Doctor. Even *you* can figure that out."

At this moment, before Berdoux could more than gasp and pull his hands away from the body, David Tremayne stood in the doorway of Steiner's cabin to take in the scene of death and the frustrated expressions on each of the faces in the small chamber. Tremayne reacted in horror, mumbled something that no one could hear and turned from the scene.

"All right, that's enough," Braddock snapped at the Russian, who was getting to his feet.

"Everyone," Kalsinov shouted to the others, "Go to your cabin! Lock yourselves in until it's time to board the 216."

Braddock caught the Russian by the arm and pulled him back. "I'm still giving the orders, Kalsinov." The Russian turned on the Captain and sneered loudly so that no one would miss his words.

"Yes," he hissed, "and we've all seen the results of those orders. Three people dead already. Are you hoping for a fourth?" Braddock tried to pour oil on the water. He was angry at Kalsinov, but thoroughly understood his irrational outburst. If he was to remain in charge of this mission, Braddock thought, now was the moment to re-establish his authority. Aloud he said in a commanding yet reassuring voice, "We'll be safer if we gather our personal belongings and wait together on the Command Deck until we depart. That way we'll all be within sight of each other."

"I disagree," shouted Kalsinov.

"Disagree all you like, Colonel," said the Captain in carefully measured tones, "but do as you are told."

The Russian and the American hooked eyeballs. It was a power play without a word, just the looks of these two strong, and if the truth be known, frightened men. The moment sustained itself for nearly a minute. The tension was broken by the Frenchman.

"I'll collect my things, Captain," he said, moving to the door of the cabin where Tremayne was still staring at the body. "David?" he said. Tremayne nodded, still in a state of shock. After a long moment, the Russian slowly got to his feet and quickly left the cabin of the dead man without another word.

CHAPTER TWENTY-THREE

"Yes, I understand," the Russian KGB agent at Mission Control was saying on the telephone. His mood was somber, his face grey. "I am not sure . . ." He sounded like he was getting instructions through an intermediary he did not altogether trust. "Will you please repeat to me the Commissar's *exact* words?" Rostov pulled at his earlobe as he listened carefully. "I see," he said at length in a reflective voice. "There is a way. It will be difficult, but I will try." For a moment, he held on to the receiver in his hand before slowly replacing it. His face appeared to be looking through the walls of the Command Center. He looked thoughtful and troubled.

In his private office, McCallister was seated in the floodlit area under the gaze of the single TV camera. On the TV screen in front of him was the unscrambled image of Captain Braddock aboard the Conestoga. Just out of camera range, a few steps behind and to the side, McCallister's chief of security sat watching and listening. Both he and McCallister looked as though they had opened letters edged in black. "How long had he been dead?" the Director asked an equally drawn face on the TV screen.

"Berdoux says an hour — two at the most — but he's unreliable," Braddock confessed. "Pamela Cooper says the doctor's suffering from some kind of tumour. His hands shake, his vision's almost gone."

McCallister took this news like it was simply the latest in a series of jabs to his midsection. He wondered when the bell would ring to signal the end of the round. Three dead bodies aboard the Space Lab and the medical man next door to being sightless. He tried to muster his thoughts and preserve some semblance of order in the investigation. "Can you reconstruct everyone's whereabouts at the time of Steiner's death?"

"What for?" Neal Braddock asked, flashing his anger across the intervening thousands of miles. "I know who killed him. It was Kalsinov." This was a shocker for McCallister. Braddock could read his chief's surprise in the monitor. He tried to explain his conviction. "Look, Andy,

Steiner was a big man — very strong. The women couldn't have done it. Berdoux's infirm and as for David . . ." He paused here and changed gears slightly. "By the way, I was able to confirm their relationship."

"They could have had a falling out," McCallister suggested.

From the sidelines, and out of camera range, Mitch Carlino added, "There's still you, Captain."

"Who said that? Mitch?" Carlino moved closer to his chief and under the watchful eye of the fixed camera.

"Captain," Carlino said, "I've got some questions I've got to ask."

"Are you suggesting that *I* killed Steiner?" said the Captain in disbelief. McCallister's attention was interrupted by the buzzing of his intercom. Dinah knew better than to call him at a time like this. He got out of his chair and hurried to his desk. Mitch moved to the centre of Braddock's screen.

"I'm not suggesting anything yet," Mitch said flatly. "But I *do* want to know about you and Olga Denerenko."

At his desk, McCallister flipped the switch on the intercom. "Dinah," he said, "you'll have to hold everything. We can't be disturbed."

Meanwhile, Braddock and Carlino had the following exchange, which McCallister watched from the desk. "I don't understand the question," said Captain Braddock.

"Come on, Captain," insisted Carlino. "Fifteen years ago. London. A party at the Soviet Embassy. *Now* do you understand the question?"

"If you've got a point to make, make it," Braddock snapped.

Dinah's voice was on the intercom. "I'm sorry, sir, but the Vice-President and Mr Rostov are here. They must see you immediately."

McCallister glanced at Mitch leaning into his interrogation of Braddock, then told Dinah, "Send them in." He turned to Carlino. "Mitch, drop it," he ordered.

At that moment, the door to McCallister's inner office opened and the Veep and Alexander Rostov moved quickly into the room. Carlino told Braddock to stand by, then got up to shake hands with the visitors after the Director greeted them.

"Andy, sorry to break in at this hour," the Vice-President said simply, "but we've got a problem." He shot a look at Carlino and added: "Guess you'd better be a part of this too, Mr Carlino." The Veep took a new breath and loomed at McCallister as he spoke. "Mr Rostov wants to speak directly with Colonel Kalsinov. I've agreed." McCallister and Carlino stood without motion. The Vice-President went towards the TV camera. "Captain Braddock?" he asked.

From the Conestoga came Braddock's voice, a little confused by the surprisingly familiar face on the screen before him. "Yes, sir?" answered the Captain. The Veep explained what was required, offering no explanations. Braddock complied. He operated his own desk speaker. "Colonel Kalsinov, please report to my cabin immediately."

While they were waiting for the Russian to arrive, McCallister used the time to bring both the Veep and Rostov up to date. "Sir," he began, "we've had another problem aboard the space lab." The Veep raised his heavy eyebrows.

"Oh?"

"By *problem*," asked Rostov, "do you mean another death?"

"Kurt Steiner was found strangled in his cabin less than thirty minutes ago." McCallister let it lie there, the simple fact of a third death.

"My God, Andy," said the Vice-President with feeling, "we've got to get those people *down*."

At this moment, on the TV screen, they could hear the door to Braddock's cabin open. Braddock gave a tight smile to the Colonel, and offered him his place in front of the automatic TV camera. He nervously made the introduction. "Mr Vice-President, Colonel Kalsinov." Kalsinov neither smiled nor scowled, he simply steeled himself for whatever was about to happen.

The Veep continued: "Colonel, I am here with Mr Rostov. He wishes to speak with you."

Rostov spoke up. He was not backward about coming forward. "In private, sir." That was a surprise. McCallister was the first to register a protest.

"No way . . ."

"Mr Vice-President, I must *protest* . . ."

The Vice-President's face removed from itself all former lines and wrinkles that suggested the familiar Veep of the press conferences and the campaign trail. This was a hard face that was not to be trifled with. "Protest all you like, Mr Rostov," he said in a voice that didn't invite an argument, "but considering what's going on up there, whatever you've got to say, we're *all* going to hear."

Rostov was a pragmatist. He had made his best effort, now there was nothing further to do but make a stuffy acceptance of the inevitable. "As you wish," he said. He turned to the familiar Russian face on the screen. "Colonel, we are obviously all concerned about this dangerous situation. Moscow has ordered me to ask you directly if you are satisfied with the leadership of Captain Braddock."

The Americans watched the two Russians facing one another. Kalsinov began his reply slowly, measuring his words before pronouncing them. "The Captain and I have disagreed often, but it would be unfair to hold him responsible for what's happening at the moment."

"Do you feel you should assume command for the remainder of the mission?" From his tone of voice, Rostov sounded not like he was asking for information that might help solve the present problems, but more like a fact-finding mission gathering data for an inquiry to be held at some later date, after the final catastrophe had removed the witness from any further possibility of recall.

"At this time," Kalsinov said in a low voice, as though he knew he was not rendering the wanted or looked-for verdict, "Captain Braddock has the confidence of the others."

"That's *not* an answer, Colonel."

"It is the best I can give you, sir."

Rostov paused as though he had something further to communicate to the cosmonaut, but he seemed to decide against it. "Very well, I'm satisfied. Best wishes for a safe re-entry," said Rostov, who then added, in a voice that was deceptively casual, "Oh, and Colonel — Premier Savarnych sends warmest personal regards." None of the Americans in McCallister's office failed to note this closing remark of the Russian. They exchanged looks. On the TV screen, McCallister watched Kalsinov's face. He thought he recognized a slight flicker of understanding in the cosmonaut's face. When he replied, he spoke carefully as though not wholly trusting his voice:

"I am grateful to the Premier."

McCallister and Carlino shared a puzzled look. Rostov got out of the chair under the baleful gaze of the TV camera and rejoined the others.

"Thank you," he said, trying to sound casual and his old ironic self once more. "I realize my request was somewhat unusual, but what Moscow proposes . . ." He didn't bother to complete his joke, but shrugged: "We all have our orders."

The Veep nodded at McCallister and Carlino,

and left the room with Rostov without further conversation. On the TV screen, McCallister saw the face of Kalsinov smile and leave the frame. In a moment the door clicked and he knew that the Russian had left the Captain's cabin. Mc-Callister was frowning, as though he could smell an unpleasant odour that he could not locate in any of the usual places.

Carlino was the first to break the silence: "Look, maybe I'm being paranoid," he said, "but why the hell is Rostov bringing best wishes from a deposed former premier for?" He looked around the room, as though there were more people filling it than just McCallister and himself. "It doesn't make any sense — " Carlino stopped himself, his face lighting up with a possibility that had just occurred to him. "Un-less . . ." he hesitated to give it utterance.

Aboard the Space Lab, the remaining cosmonaut walked back to his cabin with a sober tread. He made the last turn, and opened the door to his cabin. Inside, Colonel Kalsinov first of all locked the door behind him. Quickly, he moved to his bunk, kneeled down and reached underneath. Into the light, he brought an attaché case, which he laid on his bunk. He opened the case and emptied the contents on the bed. With a penknife taken from his pocket, Kalsinov cut away the bottom of the case, revealing a false bottom. The Colonel breathed heavily at the secrecy, if not the effort, required to rip away the still-intact leather. Nestled in the contoured hiding place was an ugly-looking machine pistol. The Russian was about to remove it, when there was a sudden rattling at the door of the cabin. "Who is there?" he demanded in anger. "Go away!" he shouted at the closed door.

Whoever it was who wanted to get in, now began banging loudly on the Russian's door.

In his own cabin, Neal Braddock was still in contact with McCallister at Mission Control. On his own screen, he could see the Vice-President. He knew that Carlino and McCallister were just beyond camera range, and would poke their heads in when required.

"Sir," Braddock was saying, "I agree with Mr Carlino. I think it's possible — even *probable* — that Rostov just gave Colonel Kalsinov a secret pre-arranged order — possibly to somehow try to take over this mission —"

Braddock never finished what he was planning to say. The sound of his voice was drowned out by the noise of a tremendous explosion aboard the Space Lab. Braddock was almost lifted from his chair, the cabin lurched as the camera itself came loose. Braddock slammed into the wall as though he'd been hit by a powerful weapon. The TV screen in McCallister's office went black. McCallister and the Vice-President looked stunned at one another. Carlino's jaw dropped open.

"My God!" was the only thing that the Director was able to say.

CHAPTER TWENTY-FOUR

Braddock saw the blood smear on the floor before he felt the pain, first as a throbbing of the temples and then as a searing, stabbing red heat above his eyes. He touched the gash that had very nearly opened his forehead as he struggled, stumbling, to his feet. The Command Deck! He moved, half bent over, along the corridor, the blare of the klaxon horn reverberating through the halls, echoing in his ears, colliding, it seemed to Braddock, with the thudding, thudding, of the pain in his head.

It was David Tremayne, the only one left on the Command Deck, to whom Braddock shouted, the sound of his voice caught and carried away by the blaring horn. "What happened?" David was at the controls, as if fighting with them, the space lab swinging and tilting, warning lights on every computer blinking crazily. And still the horn blared.

"We've got damage, sir," Tremayne yelled, not taking his eyes off the computer panel, his hands and fingers moving across it ceaselessly. "Quadrant B3! We're losing oxygen, electric — I can't maintain stabilization!"

Braddock was off again, this time toward quadrant B3, the source of the explosion. He raced down the corridor, using his hands against the corridor walls to steady himself as the ship pitched and yawed from side to side. Suddenly Berdoux appeared, his face blackened, his head bleeding, staggering, groping along the wall. "Doctor!" Braddock shouted. "What happened?"

"I — I'm not sure," was Berdoux's answer.

Braddock had reached for Berdoux, helping him to stand, when he heard footsteps running toward them. It was Pamela, from the direction Berdoux had come. She was sweating, gasping for breath. "Kalsinov's dead!" burst out of her. "Someone blew up his cabin!"

Braddock made a move. "He may still be alive!" But Pamela grabbed his arm hard. "No!" she yelled, then, shaking her head, her voice becoming calm, "There's nothing left. I sealed the corridor. There's nothing we can do." It was at that moment that she suddenly saw Berdoux, by now sinking to the floor, the blood flowing more heavily from his ugly head wound. "Philippe!" She knelt beside him, a sob caught in her throat. "You're hurt —"

"No, no . . ." Berdoux insisted weakly, struggling to stand, failing. "I'm all right — "

"Doctor," Braddock interrupted, "I asked you — *what happened?*"

"You bastard!" Pamela suddenly screamed, hysterical, flailing her fists against Braddock's chest. "Leave him alone! He can't see."

Grabbing Pamela's wrists, steadying her, Braddock asked, "Are you *sure?*" But it was Berdoux who spoke: "I was trying to get into my cabin. Suddenly, there was an explosion. I was knocked to the ground."

The scene was all at once interrupted by a new voice. It was Dominica, racing toward the three from the direction of the Command Deck. "Captain," she screamed, "we're off trajectory! David says we're going to hit the atmosphere dead on." She stopped right in front of Braddock, she was staring at him, her eyes wide, her head cocked as if hearing a far off sound. "He can't correct our course," she whispered. In a situation that had raised all of the possible things that could go on, scanning every cranny of horror and death, suddenly there was yet one more terrible possibility to torture them. It seemed too cruel, but it was real.

McCallister was already shouting as he raced into the Communications Center, Carlino and the Vice-President following. "I want picture and sound from that space lab," he demanded of the technician, "now!"

"Sorry, sir! We've lost them!"

"Keep trying!" McCallister ordered, when another technician, a woman in a blue dress, manning the console on the far wall, said, "Doctor, they've got a massive malfunction. They're losing everything!" McCallister was already standing over her, his eyes reading the story told by the computer bank's readouts, as she went on: "They're off trajectory! If they don't correct, in about four minutes they're going to hit Earth's atmosphere like a brick wall."

"Everybody move! Into the Delta!" Braddock was ordering the five remaining crew members.

"What about the bodies?" asked Dominica.

"There isn't time!" Braddock yelled. "David! Forget it — move! Let's go!"

David turned away from the console to join the others as they headed for the hatch to Delta 216. It was Braddock who reached the hatch door first. It was Braddock who hit the switch. Nothing happened. He hit it again.

"Damn it," Braddock muttered. "She won't open!"

Pamela was starting to scream. "We're not getting any power! The electrical system's shorted out!"

David looked at his watch, then back at the console. "We're not going to make it!"

McCallister was giving orders to the technician at the main communications computer again. He'd understood immediately what Braddock

had to do: "He's got to be going for the Delta."
He asked the technician, "Can you establish
radio contact?"

"No, sir," was the answer. "The Delta's system
won't receive until they've entered Earth's atmosphere."

McCallister sucked in a breath: "Hook onto
the primary frequency and start sending."

"I'm going to the back-up system," Braddock
shouted above the blare of the horn. "Everybody
into the corridor — down on the floor!" And the
four crew members, David and Berdoux being
helped by Pamela and Dominica, crept toward
the corridor, hunkering on the floor.

Braddock, carefully but quickly, reached
down to open a lid set into the floor beside the
hatchway. He had his hand on the red handle
that lay beneath as David said smartly, "You've
got three seconds, sir." Braddock leaned over the
handle, his fingers encircling it, a small tug and
then — as he yanked it, Braddock took three
leaps and then dived to the floor, protected
behind the console as the hatch lid to Delta 216
exploded open.

"Let's go," Braddock said between tight lips,
and the five surviving astronauts, each in turn,
entered Delta 216 from the hatchway above it.

It was Braddock who slipped behind the controls, Pamela came next, with Berdoux leaning
on her shoulder. Then Dominica, and then
David, securing the interior hatch behind him

and slipping into the co-pilot's seat next to Braddock.

"We got enough fuel in this thing to make
it from here?" Braddock asked, not looking at
David.

"We're sure as hell going to find out," the
young Tremayne answered.

The two men began, with a kind of dance-like
rhythm, to throw the switches, pull the stops,
flip gears.

"Power, activated," Braddock said.

"Check," David answered.

"Turbos, activated."

"Check."

"Separation."

"Separation confirmed."

A moment's pause, then Braddock: "Ignition." There was no answer as David continued
to manipulate the panel switches. "Ignition!"
Braddock repeated, loud and hard this time. A
green light flashed on the console. "Ignition,
confirmed," David said.

And with a "Let's go" from Braddock, the
small red Delta 216 dropped down the underbelly of the Conestoga Space Lab, then blasted
forward, winging into space.

CHAPTER TWENTY-FIVE

The Communications Center was busy. Technicians were deployed at computer terminals in
curved rows. The rounded walls of this, the
nerve centre of Mission Control now, under the
indirect lighting, made the architect's vision of
the centre come true. Activity brought the place
to life. Only when all positions were working flat
out did the symmetry of the design make perfect
sense. McCallister felt at home here, surrounded
by the best ground crew that could be assembled
anywhere. Still, every once and a while, he had
to remind himself that with all of this hardware
and technicians representing billions of dollars,
they were collectively helpless to effect the smallest alteration in the Delta's course. They could

calculate the smallest variation from normal operating procedures, but they could only alert the crew to their findings and then hope.

McCallister was looking over the shoulder of the chief radar technician. "Sir," he said, turning to the Director, "I've got a blip coming off the Space Lab. I think they've launched the Delta." McCallister patted the man lightly on the shoulder, and moved to the panel that controlled the large TV screen.

"Put the trajectory grid up on the screen."

"Yes, sir." The technician put down his clipboard and hit several buttons. Suddenly the screen was filled with a radar grid with a blip slowly moving across it, leaving a red trail in its wake.

"Howard," the Director said, "give me a trajectory calculation." The technician hit several more buttons, which brought a green line to the picture. It was running close to the red path of the blip, but it was far enough away to furrow McCallister's brow.

"No good, Doctor! They're way off!" McCallister moved back to the first technician.

"Have they got the capability to correct?"

"It's possible, but they're running out of time." The face of this and every other technician on the floor was grim. It was going to be a near run thing, if they could bring it off at all.

Meanwhile, aboard the Delta 216, David Tremayne was pushing buttons and reading printouts of his own. Seeing the bad news of the trajectory calculations, he punched in some corrective data. Almost to himself he said, "We're coming in shallow. We're going to bounce off." Captain Braddock looked at the same readout. He, too, was wearing a grim expression.

"Fuel's at four-six percent," he said and added his interpretation of the evidence. "We haven't got enough for a second pass."

David nodded. It was now or never. "Correcting forward attitude to six-oh-eight-niner-*now*."

Immediately behind Braddock and Tremayne sat the remaining crew members, already strapped into their contoured seats with a clear view of the control panels. There were three empty seats alongside them, and an additional chair at the control section. Berdoux looked confused and tired. Pamela reached over and took his hand, squeezing it comfortingly. Dominica looked straight ahead of her.

Like the five astronauts, McCallister back at Mission Control was watching the TV screen with a desperate intensity, his gaze fixed on the two projected trajectories. There was only the slight flicker of his eyelid — of hope? — as he saw the red line start to rise and change shape, now more nearly conforming to the green line.

Standing behind McCallister were Carlino and the Vice-President, whose eyes went from the screen to McCallister's face and then, with a questioning look, to Carlino. "The red line,"

Carlino whispered in explanation, "is the Delta's course, sir. The green line is the correct trajectory for re-entry." The Veep was nodding. "If they can put the two together, they'll make it back."

The red line rose and curved again. "Come on, baby," McCallister said tensely under his breath, "come on —"

"Twenty-nine seconds to atmosphere," Howard, the chief radar technician, announced. Slowly, slowly, the red line continued to conform, as all eyes were fixed on the giant screen. "Ten seconds to go," the technician went on, "nine — eight —" A sharp intake of breath from McCallister was heard as the count continued; Carlino's lean body tensed, and the Veep clenched his fists, sweat breaking out on his brow. "Five — four — three — two — one — mark."

Suddenly, the red line had disappeared from the screen.

"What happened?" the Vice-President asked anxiously.

Carlino's voice was shaky. "They've lost radar contact in the ionization belt."

"Did they make it?"

"We'll know in a minute."

McCallister had moved across to the second technician, listening intently as she continued her attempt to contact the Delta crew: "Delta, this is Control. Do you read? Delta, this is Control, please acknowledge." She waited for the contact. Nothing. "Delta," she said again, "this is Control. Do you read? Please acknowledge."

Silence was the only answer, broken only by McCallister's "Come on, *answer*, dammit — *answer!*" A technician turned up the gain on the receiving circuits to amplify the faintest sound. The tension in the control room mounted. Nothing. Nothing but silence.

Then suddenly, a loud crackle of static. It was a voice — Braddock's voice — coming through: "Control, this is Delta, we read you loud and clear. We're coming home!" he shouted as pandemonium, cheers and crying broke out in the control room. The grin that broke across McCallister's face was like a sudden dawn at midnight, and the Director laughed as he was hugged by one technician, then another. The nod exchanged between Carlino and McCallister was one that knew all the risks taken, the hopes, fears and dangers.

As McCallister now went to join Carlino and the Vice-President, the Veep congratulated him with a smile and a handshake. "Helluva job, Andy. Thank God, they're coming in safe."

McCallister grunted. "*Five* of them, sir," he reminded the politician; then, turning to Carlino: "Mitch, I want a jet ready in thirty minutes to fly to Edwards. I also want security at the base tripled. Nobody in or out."

Carlino nodded, understanding, but the Veep was puzzled: "What is it, McCallister? You know something, don't you?"

"No, sir, right now I'm just guessing."

"You want to share your thoughts?"

"Not yet, sir. Not just yet." Carlino and the

Veep watched, as McCallister turned and left the room. On his way to what? the Veep wondered.

Carlino tried to imagine the Delta 216 speeding towards planet Earth. He could picture the outline, but the details were indistinct, as though they were obscured by the questions that were overriding his imagination. He paused and let the space vehicle stop in his mind, so as to concentrate on those insistent questions:

> Who killed Olga Denerenko?
> Who killed Guy Sterling?
> Who killed Kurt Steiner?
> Who killed Andrei Kalsinov?

Could you become the *Whodunit?* Detective of the Year?

Do you know *who* killed Olga Denerenko, Guy Sterling, Kurt Steiner and Andrei Kalsinov?

If you believe you do, you could become our *Whodunit?* Detective of the Year.

Using the following entry form, send us your solution to the murders. In the section *Who?* write the name or names of the person(s) you believe killed each individual. Then suggest an apt and original name for future international manned space missions, made up from initial letters – e.g., International Mission To Explore Space (I.M.T.E.S.) – using not more than 12 words.

Whodunit? Murder in Space will first be shown by the Independent Television Network on the evening of Tuesday 13 August 1985. You then have 10 days to work out the mystery and send in your solution. Only after all the entries are in will the screenplay be taken from the bank vault in Los Angeles, the actors assembled, and Part Two of this dramatic cliffhanger shot for airing worldwide in mid-September. This part two show will play in front of an invited audience, selected from those competition entrants who send in the correct solution, at Central Television's Nottingham Studios in mid-September when the *Whodunit?* Detective of the Year will be chosen. Final contestants will be questioned, amongst other things, on how and why the murders were committed.

Can you solve the mystery of *Murder in Space*? Send your entry to *Whodunit?*, PO Box 4WH, London W1A 4WH postmarked not later than last post on Friday 23 August.

Rules

1. The competition is open to UK residents except employees of Zenith Productions, any ITV Contractor, or Penguin Books, and their families.

2. The entry instructions are deemed to form part of the rules of the contest.

3. All entries will be examined by a panel of judges which will contain at least one independent judge.

4. All entries become the property of Zenith Productions Ltd, and will not be returned. The judges' decision is final and correspondence will not be entered into.

5. There are no cash prizes, and expenses claims from contestants who opt to travel to Nottingham will not be entertained.

6. The names of the studio contestants and the solution will be revealed on air in mid-September, and to contestants who send an s.a.e. to the competition address.

WHO?

OLGA DENERENKO

GUY STERLING

KURT STEINER

ANDREI KALSINOV

My choice of name for the space mission is......................

....

NAME: ....

ADDRESS: ....

....

....

....

AGE: ....

TEL NO: ....

Have you made any previous TV appearances?
Are you available, if requested, to visit our Nottingham Studios
on 14 September?

**Please write the name of the person(s) you believe killed
Olga Denerenko on the back flap of the envelope contain-
ing your entry form.**